HOPE REDEEMED

A SPANISH NOVELLA

OF GOLD & BLOOD

BOOK SIX

Jenny Wheeler

ISBN 978-0-473-49840-5 (Paperback)
ISBN 978-0-473-49841-2 (epub)
ISBN 978-0-473-49842-9 (Kindle)

OF GOLD & BLOOD SERIES

Poisoned Legacy #1

Brother Betrayed #2

Double Jeopardy #3

Tangled Destiny – A Christmas Novella and Prequel #4

Unbridled Vengeance #5

Hope Redeemed – A Spanish Novella #6

Tardé una hora en conocerte y solo un día en enamorarme. Pero me llevará toda una vida lograr olvidarte.

It took me an hour to get to know you and just a day to fall in love. But it will take me a whole life to be able to forget you. *Anon., popularized by Acción Poética.*

1

"Do I have to?"

Caleb Stewart's — and Rancho Del Oro's — head vaquero Santiago Valaquez warily eyed the baby bundle his cousin held out to him, the child's newborn form obscured by the frothy fall of the lace-edged christening gown. The reluctance signaled by his twisted mouth was contradicted by the impudent sparkle in his hazel eyes as he challenged Francine's gaze.

She broke into her characteristic bubbly giggle, her auburn curls bobbing with joy as she handed the child over. "You most certainly do. You're *el padrino*, after all."

Francine Esterhazy thrust the white-gowned infant toward him, her face glowing pink with a new mother's pride. "If you're not careful, I'll insist you're photographed with him, as well. I know how you'd just love that."

Giggles overflowed once more. "Our son and heir is in safe hands with you as godfather, Santiago. I know it."

He felt a warmth in his chest. The one thing he wanted to do today was get through the occasion without causing embarrassment to those closest to him — Francine and her mother, his Aunt Benecio. Being shut up in an ornate room in a dinner jacket was so far outside his normal territory he had to keep reminding himself to relax.

Francine wreathed her arm lightly around the back of his neck and leaned in. Her breath was warm on his cheek. "It's so wonderful to see you again, Santiago. It's been far too long."

They'd grown up together in an extended Los Angeles family compound shared with aunts and uncles, cousins and "orphans" like him. Francine and he were cousins rather than siblings, Francine's mother, his Aunt Benecio, having raised him from birth after his mother Luisa — Benecio's youngest sister — died in labor. But he'd always regarded her as his half-sister.

They had a special bond that felt closer than mere cousins, with him three years older and always looking out to protect Francine from her older brother Leo. When they reached their teens, life carried them in very different directions, and he'd seen very little of Francine for the last few years.

Santiago gazed down at the baby boy's calm, milky-blue eyes and was gripped with a sudden solemn sense of responsibility.

"I can't believe it. My little 'sister' married to one of the California wine kings, and a mother as well. You're really leaving me and Leo in the dust." He grinned in an attempt to recapture their earlier gaiety, but Francine's eyes sharpened.

"About that, Antal wants to talk to you later. We both think you should put your vaquero days behind you. Start building yourself more of a future."

The baby in his arms wriggled and gave a little cry. Santiago mimicked rocking cradle movements for a few seconds before thrusting him awkwardly back to Francine.

"Charlie needs his mother. And don't worry about me. I'm fine."

The buttery yellow walls of the Esterhazy's spacious reception room seemed to throb with the chatter from the extended tribe gathered to celebrate the arrival of Charles Frederick Esterhazy, scion of wine-making Hungarian nobility now thoroughly settled in California. And in case anyone forgot the family's origins, the chandelier-lit room, its high walls punctuated by deep arched windows and topped by gilded crown moldings, were reminder enough of the enviable wealth and social status the Esterhazys had brought with them to the Golden State.

Santiago pivoted on his heel and wondered if it was too early to steal away. A quick survey of the room showed Caleb and his French fiancée Madeleine standing near the string quartet in animated discussion with Caleb's sister Josefa. They were here because Caleb's Vino d'Oro winery venture shared common interests with Antal and Francine's Orleans Hill winery. He guessed the two men would be talking viticulture over cigars later.

Santiago moved across the room to join them, his heart lifting at the sight of Josefa's grave face, her dark eyes gazing out from under strong, arched brows. Her generous mouth quirked at his approach.

They'd got close over the last winter, no doubt about it, as Josefa had wrestled with coming to terms with the violent death of Rory Mackinnon, her beloved betrothed. As he closed the gap between them, he reminded himself yet again that "close" was as far as it would ever go.

He'd fallen into his familiar pattern, protective of her just as he'd been of Francine. But she was an heiress, sharing in a family heritage of a 5000-acre ranch dating back to the days of the old Spanish land grants. He was a lowly ranch hand, a footloose and fancy-free vaquero, with nothing to offer by way of money or prospects.

"My word, Santiago. You polish up well, don't you?" Madeleine smiled up at him from her aquamarine eyes. "You'll be turning all the ladies' heads in that dinner jacket."

Before he could respond, Leo appeared at Josefa's side. "Really?

Good old Santiago? I wouldn't think he'd be anything to write home about." Leo attempted to disarm the barb with an ingenuous smile, but the chatter chilled to awkward silence.

After a moment, Santiago realized that the others may not have formally met Leo. He'd have to do the honors. He suppressed a surge of irritation and gestured toward his cousin.

"Oh, sorry. Caleb Stewart and Madeleine Laurent. Meet Leo Carver." Leo stepped forward to shake Caleb's hand and proffer a slight bow to Madeleine. Santiago gestured to Josefa. "And Caleb's sister, Josefa Stewart. Leo Carver."

Leo stepped forward and took up Josefa's hand. He brushed his lips across it lightly and held it for a moment before gently letting it go again. Josefa's eyes widened.

"The unparalleled Miss Stewart. Word of your beauty precedes you and is not exaggerated." His face puckered in sympathy and he added more quietly, "Allow me to offer my heartfelt sympathy for your recent loss."

Josefa's eyes flickered uncertainly, and Santiago's chest felt as if someone had thrust a knife into it.

Caleb stepped in to cover the awkwardness. "So, Mr. Carver, you're Francine's brother? Do you have any involvement with Orleans Hill?"

"No, no, definitely not." He shot Santiago a challenging look. "I'm not a man of the land. Not at all, I'm afraid. I prefer easier ways of getting my hands dirty, so to speak." He flashed a weak grin at Caleb. "I'm a lawyer with property and business interests in San Francisco."

He turned to Josefa. "Would you do me the honor of taking a stroll in the garden, Miss Stewart? I very much wish to learn more of your interests. I feel certain we'd find we have something in common."

After a moment's hesitation Josefa nodded and offered him her arm. "Charmed, I'm sure, Mr. Carver. I believe Antal's glasshouses are something to behold."

Santiago fought the urge to bunch his fists as the pair strolled away. The pain in his chest intensified. "Nice for Josefa to get out and about," he said to Caleb. "She's had a horrible time the last few months. It will do her good."

Caleb's returning gaze told him he didn't believe a word of what he'd said. And neither did he.

2

Leo Carver's face was oval. His olive skin matched his raven-dark hair and hooded eyes. As he led Josefa from the reception room, she shot him a side-long glance. His expression revealed nothing of what he might be thinking. Nothing at all. Josefa couldn't decide whether that made him mysterious and exciting, or shifty and questionable.

As they left the crowd behind, they caught a refreshing waft of cool air as they passed by a small sitting room. The door was ajar and Francine sat with her back turned from full view, a white bundle cradled in her arms. Her husband hovered at her shoulder, everything about his stance indicating he was on tenterhooks to offer his wife any kind of service she might desire.

Josefa swallowed back the hard lump that rose in her throat at the sight of them. That could have been her. Raising her child with Rory, her one true love. He would have been a wonderful father, she knew it. Just as he was a caring lover. And now, because of a horrible trick of fate, she would have to go through with bearing and raising their child alone. No loving man, no caring father at her side.

Unless she managed to find one before too much longer. She steeled her heart. It could never again be like it was with Rory, she knew that. But maybe she could make a business-like marriage. Such arrangements were common in the Californio world. There hadn't been a big age difference between her parents, but her Mexican mother and Scottish father had enjoyed a very happy union until Fergus Stewart's too-early death. And there'd certainly been a business aspect to it — the Spanish grant had come through her family, not his.

In that world, young girls were often married off to much older, well-to-do men. And from what she'd seen, the marriages often worked well for both parties. She could think of several such arrangements in her wider family circle that had been highly successful partnerships, the wives even assuming family business interests after their older husbands died.

"You're awfully quiet. A penny for your thoughts."

Leo halted his progress to the conservatory and held her arm out, one hand supporting it underneath, the other caressing. Stroking, stroking. Very gently on top.

She felt unaccustomed tears spring to her eyes.

No! This is dreadful! I am not going to cry in public. And especially not in front of this handsome, single man.

She squeezed her eyes shut and cleared her throat. "Oh, nothing. Really. Do let's find some fresh air."

They progressed along the open paths and into the conservatory, marveling at the unusual plants Antal's gardeners were propagating under glass. South American tomatoes and pawpaws. Big desert cacti. Espaliered pears and apples and, of course, many varieties of grapes.

And then Leo propelled her to a corner bench, invited her to rest, and launched in. "Josefa. Forgive me, dear lady, for getting right to the point. But there is something about you, something strong and calculating, that makes me think you will appreciate a direct approach."

He took her right hand and once again lightly brushed it with his lips. A strange little shiver ran up her spine.

"I always consider business — successful business — very romantic. And I think we could do very successful business together."

Again, a weird little tingle ran through her. *Who is this man? Some sort of shaman?*

When she responded she sounded breathless. "Business? What sort of business?"

"The best kind." He pushed up beside her, so their thighs touched on the bench. He reached over and gently turned her face towards his. "The sort that combines business and pleasure." And he leaned over and kissed her, the barest brushing of his lips across hers.

The moment hung in time. Never had she known such a small movement to have such a breathtaking impact. She stared at him, hardly believing what he'd just done, the tingling running up her arms, down her back. Her head was buzzing. *The man is a sorcerer.*

She rose slowly, one hand still lightly clasped in his.

"Mr. Carver," she said. "Please explain yourself."

His eyes flicked to her waistline, then he waved his free hand in a sinuous line. "Miss Stewart, I believe it is generally recognized in your private circles, very private circles I assure you, that you are, shall we say, in a compromised situation?"

He lifted one eyebrow. He looked like a pirate, she thought. Not like a San Francisco lawyer at all. And he was as relentless as she imagined a pirate would be.

"I expect you would appreciate your situation being, shall we say, regularized as soon as it possibly can be. Certainly well before the birth of your child."

Josefa sat down again with a gasp, and he stroked his index finger lightly across the top of her arm as he continued to talk, drawing mesmerizing figures of eight on the thin fabric of her sleeve.

"I would propose that we come to an arrangement. Your brother settles a generous dowry on you, in return for which we will wed and give your child a respectable name. In return, I will settle a share of my substantial estate on you. We both benefit, and your child does too."

He patted her arm comfortingly. "If anything, heaven forbid, should happen to me, you and your child would be well-provided for life. And likewise, if anything happened to you, I would have the security of knowing the child had his own legacy for his education and care."

He appeared delighted at his own cleverness. "What do you think?"

What did she think? The truth was, she couldn't think. She sat dumbfounded, staring at him. She jerked her arm away, suddenly irritated by the hypnotizing touch.

"I think this is all rather sudden and unexpected, Mr. Carver. Do you really expect me to give you an answer right now?"

"Not right now, no, of course not. But I think you'd agree, you haven't got a lot of time to spare, do you?"

3

"Antal, I appreciate the offer. I do."

Santiago scanned the crowd around him, checking they weren't in danger of being overheard. Josefa hadn't returned from her stroll with Leo. Caleb and Madeleine were perched in a comfortable corner taking coffee with Benecio. He should join them. He hadn't had a chance to do much more than greet his aunt, and she was looking so much older than he remembered.

He ran his finger around his collar, which suddenly felt as if it was half-choking him. As Francine had hinted he would, her husband had drawn him aside and made him a generous offer.

Santiago leaned his elbow on a small bar set up at the far end of the room, deep in a man-to-man heart-to-heart conversation, pausing occasionally to savor the warmth of the brandy as it slipped easily down his throat.

"Come and work for Orleans Hill as assistant cellar manager," Antal had said, "and we'll train you up in all aspects of viticulture."

The money he was offering was half again what he was being paid at the ranch. And he'd still be spending a good part of his working day outside among the grapes.

Antal Esterhazy clapped a brotherly hand on his shoulder. "I know you love the open range, Santiago, and I'm sure you're a great asset to Del Oro. But you have to ask yourself, do you really want to spend the rest of your life as head vaquero on someone else's outfit?

"This way you've got an opportunity to build a future. If you take to it, and learn the business, Francine and I will cut you in on a share in a few years. You'll have a chance to make something of yourself."

Santiago felt the color rising in his cheeks. He hated the feeling that he was some sort of family project.

Poor old Santiago. He'll never amount to anything. Is that what they thought? Even worse, were they right?

Antal grasped his hand, as though he was reading his mind. "This isn't some family favor, Santiago."

He gestured to the empty bar stools and perched his rear on one. "Sure, Francine thinks the world of you. That's true. And we all know you got a rough deal after Benecio married Leo's father. There are some wrongs there that deserve to be righted. But if that was all there was to it, we wouldn't be talking. You've proved yourself a capable manager of men. Tough but fair. We'll be getting someone we know who can do the job, someone we trust. And believe you me, these days, that means a lot."

Santiago edged his butt onto the stool facing Antal and sighed. "It's a great offer, Antal. Really, it is."

He wondered why his heart wasn't doing cartwheels in gratitude. Everything Antal said was right. So why did a heaviness open up in the pit of his stomach at the thought of leaving Del Oro?

He loved the freedom of the range, the escape with the wind in his face. He didn't have to think about the nastiness, the stifling mess he'd left behind at Benecio's. At Del Oro he could pretend none of it had ever happened.

He leaned back and surveyed the room again, thinking of how to respond.

Josefa and Leo had returned. They were slowly moving towards the corner where Benecio held court, but had been intercepted by a tall man who apparently had something he wanted to tell Leo. Josefa's arm was firmly glued to his, and they were walking in step, looking already as though they'd forged some sort of alliance.

"Antal, just give me a couple of days to think things through. I'll need to talk to Caleb. You've been extremely generous, and I'd be a fool to turn you down." He grinned sheepishly. "But you know me. A creature of habit. Once I find my patch, I don't like to leave it. Just give me a few days to get used to the idea."

A bright woman's voice cut through the general chatter and Francine bore down upon them.

"You've had a chance to talk? Good. And what do you think, Santiago?"

Antal pecked his wife on the cheek. "He was just saying he'll give it serious thought. What do you reckon, Santiago? Could you give us an answer, say by the end of the week? If you don't come over, we'll have to extend our search."

"End of the week? Sure. That should be plenty of time."

4

"Just so you know, Caleb. I've made a formal offer. I'm talking about Josefa and me. In business and in life. She hasn't given me an answer yet, but I'm highly optimistic."

Leo Carver gave Josefa a conspiratorial look and squeezed her arm for all to see. He smiled smugly at Caleb. "She'd be a fool to turn me down, don't you think?"

Josefa's expression was unreadable. She quietly unlinked her arm and surreptitiously increased the distance between herself and the insufferably confident attorney.

Caleb's mouth momentarily dropped open, as if he couldn't believe his ears. Then he quickly regained his composure.

"Really, Leo? A rather unconventional approach for a lawyer, I'd suggest. But I suppose the circumstances might require . . ."

His voice trailed off as he regarded his sister. "Are you okay, Josefa?"

"Perfectly fine," she replied in a clipped tone, sinking into a space on the sofa next to Benecio.

Santiago had been standing behind Benecio, hoping to draw her aside for a quiet chat, when Josefa and Leo had reappeared. He felt as if he was invisible, falling off the edge of his known world. He gripped the back of the sofa, as if to reassure himself he was actually present. *Josefa and Leo? They've known each other three minutes!*

When Josefa spoke, her voice had a breathy quality, as if she too was in a state of shock. "There are some matters we'll need to discuss, Caleb. As Leo says, this is a business proposition."

Caleb frowned. "I see. Anything to see you settled and happy, Josefa. As soon as we get home, we can talk."

5

Santiago wanted out. As soon as possible, if not right now, because being at Rancho Del Oro — particularly anywhere near Leo and Josefa — was intolerable.

Since they'd come home from Charles Esterhazy's christening two days ago, Leo had been staying at the ranch, getting to know Josefa better and conducting whatever negotiations he deemed necessary with Caleb, who wore a constantly harried expression.

Santiago had no idea what they were talking about, and he didn't want to. He just wanted to stay clear of them all.

The dull ache in his heart when he thought of Josefa marrying the man who had ruined his childhood couldn't be ignored. He didn't know what upset him more: that Leo was the man Josefa seemed to have lined up, or that she was getting married to anyone except him.

Because now that he was confronted with the brutal reality — Josefa needed a husband — the more he saw he was nowhere in the running.

He had nothing to offer of either substance or status. She was the granddaughter of a noted Spanish house, the daughter and sister of a substantial run-holder, and he was a cowboy who ran a team.

The more he pondered his situation, the more clearly he saw what he had to do. His best option, his only option really, was to accept Antal's offer of a position at Orleans Hill and move on as soon as he could.

It was with that very thought in mind, his limbs pleasantly fatigued from a day in the saddle, that he made for the house as long shadows sloped across the yard, seeking out Caleb to hand in his resignation.

Caleb was in the small sitting room off the main family area they used as a de facto office, sitting back in his chair behind the desk with a vague, dazed expression.

"Santiago! Come in, come in. It'll be good to talk to someone with his feet on the ground. Please, please. How's it going out there? I've hardly had a chance to think about the stock for the last couple of days."

He drew his arm across his brow and gestured to the door. "Close it, will you?"

Santiago pulled the door closed behind him and sank into the chair in front of Caleb, his fingers twitching. He'd been Caleb's right-hand man for the last seven years, an apprentice vaquero for three years before that. Ten years in all. He'd felt so accepted as part of the household here under Stewart matriarch Doña Valentina's strict but kind attention he'd never imagined being anywhere else. *Funny how quickly things can change.*

When he'd turned up at Del Oro as a thin, shy seventeen-year-old desperate for work, Josefa had been an annoying thirteen-year-old who pestered everyone to go riding with her. She'd been close enough to Francine in age for him to feel comfortable in her company, and she quickly became one of the few people around whom he could be himself.

"This damn business with Josefa and Leo. It's driving me nuts."

Caleb rubbed the side of his face with a distracted air. "I don't know if I'm coming or going."

Santiago gave a reluctant nod. He didn't want to know anything about it.

"I've only just cottoned onto it, Santiago. But you know Leo well, right? You grew up with him?"

Santiago nodded even more reluctantly.

"So what do you make of him?"

The vaquero shook his head. "Oh, I'm not the one to ask. We never got on."

Caleb's eyes settled on him with pin-prick focus, the distracted air gone. "Oh? Why was that?"

Because he's a first-class bastardo? An obnoxious jerk?

Santiago shrugged. "Don't know. I was a couple of years older than he was. I was treated like a son in the house until he came along. Then I became the poor relation and he was the son and heir." He shrugged again. "You'd think he'd be happy with that, but he never let up on reminding me I was *ilegitemo.*"

"Oh? I'm sorry, Santiago. I had no idea. If you'd rather not talk about it . . ."

Santiago set his head to one side and regarded his boss.

"It's fine. I never knew my father. He was a married man. I don't even know who he was. My mother was an innocent, the youngest daughter. Benecio's sister, as you know. She died when I was born. If she'd lived — well, who knows? She'd probably have had an awful life. Everything was fine while Benecio was single and looking after me as the maiden aunt, but after she married, things changed."

He stood up, suddenly uncomfortable in his seat. "Look, Leo's got the pedigree. Good family. Money. Education. He's not particularly nice if you get on the wrong side of him, but that's not a cardinal sin, is it?"

He fixed his gaze on Caleb. "Anyway, I didn't come here to talk about Leo. I wanted to tell you. Antal's offered me a job at Orleans Hill, and I think I'll take it. I wanted to let you know, to offer my resignation."

6

Caleb stared, his jaw slack.

"What brought this on? I thought you were happy here."

"I am, mi amigo. Very happy. But things are changing. The world. Changing so fast. Ranching is changing. You know it yourself. Miller and Lux — and the other big beef operations — they're turning it into an industry, and the vaqueros are becoming factory workers. You and I are almost yesterday's men and we've barely reached thirty. I've got to think about how I'm going to ever support a family." He stared at his boss, willing him to understand. "You're all set up here, Caleb. You're about to marry Madeleine, set up your own household. It's not like that for me. Antal and Francine got me thinking, and they're right. I can't spend any more time on horseback if I'm going to amount to anything. They've said they'll make me a partner if I put in the time and learn the business. That's just too good an offer to refuse."

Caleb rose from his desk, shook his head. "We could give you a job at the vineyard if you want to get into wine. Santiago . . ."

Is Caleb pleading? Santiago just stared back, not speaking.

"Damn it, Santiago, I don't want to lose you." Caleb flicked a wary look toward the door and lowered his voice. "Especially now, with this business with Josefa."

Santiago felt the heat of rising impatience. "What business with Josefa? I don't know what you're getting at."

Caleb sighed. "You know the predicament she's got herself into. Even before this Leo thing reared its head, I'd been talking with mother about settling some of the ranch on her in a trust, so she's got some independence. I know she's desperate for some recognition of her place here.

"Under the old Spanish laws — you know, like when my parents married — women could own property independently of their husband. Since the Yanks took over California and started pushing English laws that's fading away.

"So I thought — well, actually my lawyer, good old Tom Halliburton suggested I should set it up as a trust, just to protect her and any children if things go wrong. Now that Leo's on the scene it's got a whole lot more complicated. Seems he's violently opposed to the idea of a trust. And Josefa doesn't seem to know what she wants to do."

He buried his head in his hands and massaged his forehead.

"Tell you what, Santiago. Let's go for a bit of a gallop to clear my head. I'll tell you all about it while we're out. Before those two turn up again. I've had about as much as I can stand."

He stood and grabbed a riding hat from a hook on the wall. "Let's get out of here."

"Get out of where?"

Josefa stood proud and tall in a carmine dress that underscored her passionate dark looks — the fall of black hair onto her shoulders, the generous mouth that was curved into a question as she blocked Caleb's exit. Standing behind her, his hand draped possessively over her right shoulder, was Leo.

In the few days since the christening she seemed to have grown in confidence. Her voice carried no sign of the frustrated complaint

Santiago heard so often from her — that life wasn't fair, that no one treated her seriously. Her direct gaze challenged her brother as an equal, someone who, despite the six-year difference in age, was entitled to expect answers.

If this was Leo's influence, it was all to the good, Santiago acknowledged grudgingly.

"Santiago and I are just going for a ride. Get some fresh air. Clear our heads."

"Caleb, you know we want to move things along here. We want to see the priest in the next few days about reading the banns. Leo can't hang around here forever. He's got work back in San Francisco."

"Sure, sure, Josefa. I understand what you're saying. I'm doing as much as I can. Halliburton is drawing up the papers. I can't do any more than that."

"Papers?" Leo interjected a sharp note. "I need to be consulted on any papers — consulted in detail."

He switched his attention from Caleb to Josefa though he still lazily traced the back edge of her dress with his index finger. He bent his face close to her ear and for a gut-wrenching moment Santiago wondered if he was going to nuzzle her ear in front of them. His stomach churned with an unpleasant sick feeling.

After a moment's hesitation, Leo pulled back. "Isn't that right, honey?"

Santiago flicked his focus to the window in the outside wall, trying to tune out proceedings inside the room. This was a private matter. It was like eavesdropping on personal secrets. It didn't concern him, and he didn't want to be here. He stepped toward the door. "I'll meet you outside Caleb. I'm not needed here."

Leo stepped aside to let him out. "No, you're certainly not. Haven't you got better things to do?"

Santiago stopped in his tracks, watching Caleb. His boss rarely lost his temper, but his pursed lips, the rising color in his face, told him this was one time when he was finding it hard to stay calm.

"That's not necessary or welcome, Leo. And for your information, the papers Halliburton is preparing are as I originally indicated. They're a settlement for Josefa's future, protected in a trust to ensure her independence."

Leo's posture stiffened, and it felt as if all the air had been sucked out of the room. The closest comparison Santiago could think of was being on horseback on an open plain immediately before a tornado struck. He took another couple of steps towards the door.

Leo's voice again stopped him in his tracks.

"And I told you that wasn't acceptable. We're not living in some Mexican colony under the latest Royal Cédula from Spain. We're living in America, in 1870, under American law. And if I'm giving your sister my name, my respectability, my status and protection, I expect all the due recognition of a husband under American law."

Leo's voice had risen in volume, and Josefa's stance stiffened. Her jaw jutted forward as she stared at Leo, her eyes wide in a chalky face.

Santiago couldn't take another step. His feet were fixed to the floor, hating the tableau as it unfolded before him, but unable to look away.

"Now look here, Leo," said Caleb. "Josefa has no need of your status. Or your respectability. She's got as much of both as she wants or needs, in her own right. What are you on about?"

"Caleb, I don't need you to—" Josefa's eyes were suspiciously bright, and her voice cracked.

Leo ignored her. "On her own? She got herself knocked up by some cowboy who got himself killed, and she doesn't need the protection of a husband? For God's sake, what sort of brotherly care is that?"

He glared at Caleb, and then Santiago, his lips peeled back to show wolfish white teeth.

Santiago flexed his hands. He wanted to step back, right back into the fray he'd moments ago been trying to escape, and lace his fingers around Leo's sinuous neck and throttle him.

Caleb's focus was on Josefa. "Josefa, I'm so sorry—"

"I don't need your pity, Caleb." Her voice was cutting. She'd moved toward Santiago as she spoke, her shoulders tense, her face gray and stony. "You men really are all as bad as one another."

As she pushed past him, Santiago caught a whiff of her familiar fragrance, an intoxicating mix of lavender and vanilla, deceptively simple and yet oh so complex. Just like the woman who wore it.

7

"Caleb, I really need to talk to you."

"It's not a good time, Santiago."

"Seems there's likely not going to be one around here anytime soon. Life goes on, and I need to move on too. I need to know — what are you going to do? Hire a new manager or promote one of the boys we've got now?"

They were sitting over the remains of a late ranch breakfast. Doña Valentina and the courting couple had gone into town, so they had the place to themselves, at least for now.

That was a relief in itself. Santiago was amazed that after his display yesterday, Josefa hadn't sent Leo packing. She was a lot stronger than he — and, he suspected, she — had realized. Obviously the prospect of settling into her own home held such strong appeal she was willing to try and work something out. Maybe she did really love Leo. He was good-looking enough.

"Still trying to think that one through. Quite honestly, I can't seem to get past the Leo negotiation."

Santiago had no idea where the negotiations rested, and he felt sorry for Caleb having to deal with this unholy mess. *But it's nothing to do with me.*

"Thing is, the more time I spend in that man's company, the more unsettled I feel about him." Caleb paused to gulp some coffee. "Something doesn't feel right. If he's so interested in Josefa, why does it matter if she retains control of her own money? They're still married. They'll share things."

Santiago pulled a wry face in agreement. "I did have similar thoughts myself. And the way he talked to her yesterday — it was brutal. I hope she's not going to hear that kind of stuff too often."

Caleb stood to take his cup to the kitchen. "Yeah, I know. That's why I need your help."

"I don't see what I can do as far as Josefa's concerned. The ranch, yes. But the animals were all fine the last time I looked."

"Nothing to do with the animals. I need you to do some digging on Leo."

Santiago's stomach lurched. "You what? Oh, come on, Caleb. I'm not any sort of Pinkerton. I'm an ordinary old vaquero. That's the beginning and end of it. You've got the wrong man."

"A not-so-ordinary vaquero, Santiago. And didn't you tell me you practically grew up with the fellow? You've got access to the people who know him best, and they'd trust you."

"I'm not so sure of that. They all know there was no love lost between us."

"If you won't do it for me, do it for Josefa. You two seemed to be getting on so well after that rescue from Consuela's."

Santiago's neck flushed pink. He could feel the warmth building under his shirt.

A few months back Rory Mackinnon's stepmother had tried to influence Josefa to give false testimony against Caleb. Between them, Santiago and his boss had plucked Josefa out of an impossible situation.

He rubbed his neck uneasily. The last thing he needed was for

Caleb to guess about his pathetic crush on his sister.

"She's a good kid who's had a hard time. It was the least I could do."

"Well, make this just one more thing. The last thing you can do for her. Just reassure me that Leo's got no nasty secrets, that I'm not turning my sister over to a bounder, and I'll let you go. I hate doing it, but I will. But only if you help with this last thing."

Santiago gulped back the last cold dregs of his breakfast coffee, banged down the cup and punched Caleb lightly on the arm. "You're a canny brar, you know that?"

Caleb laughed. "Oh, Santiago, I'm going to miss you. I've come to rely on you like a brar, you know that?"

Santiago grinned at him over his cup. "So where do you want me to start?"

Caleb's face was suddenly serious. "Wherever you can. Right away. Just one thing, Santiago. For goodness sake don't let on to Josefa what you're doing. She'd skin us both alive if she thought we were spying on her future husband."

8

The warm breath from a couple of dozen quietly chatting women had steamed up the coffee house windows, giving Josefa an unfamiliar sense of safety. A crazy, darting thought came to her. Nothing bad would happen while she was here enjoying a coffee with her mother. She smiled at Doña Valentina over her cup.

"You don't have to marry him, you know. There will be other opportunities." Josefa was struck by how much gray hair showed at her mother's temples. Sometime in the last little while, when she hadn't been looking, her mother had aged. And softened. A gentle smile washed across her lips. Her mother was being kind. That was unusual for the normally austere matriarch.

"Mother, are you all right? You're not sick?"

Her mother chuckled. "I'm fine, daughter. Why do you ask?"

"You just seem . . . Well, more understanding than I expected. I wouldn't blame you if you wanted me married at any cost. I mean, you have the right to be furious with me. You've 'made your bed' etcetera."

Valentina smiled, her full face lighting up. "Josefa, don't talk like that. The most important thing now is your future. I don't want you to do something that will leave you unhappy for years to come."

She put up her hand in an arresting moment. "And I am not saying marrying Leo is right or wrong. I'm just saying he is not your only option. You don't need to feel you're being backed into a corner."

Josefa nodded and sat back from the table. She glanced around the coffee house. Almost every table was filled with ladies like her mother and her, genteel women who filled the air with the sedate hum of shared feminine confidences.

"I think I know what you're getting at, Mother. I can imagine having a very good life in San Francisco with Leo. Mixing with the wives of his friends, meeting in places like this. And then he says or does something that makes me wonder if it's all wishful thinking."

Her mother's face sobered. "The thing I am most concerned about is your inheritance, girl. His attitude there — well, it's unconscionable. If it's so important to him to be the protective husband, then surely he'd be delighted to take on that task, rather than making such a ruckus about getting his hands on your endowment.

"It really goes against the grain. You know that before the Americans took over, lots of our women were given land grants — with or without their husband's name on the title. Some of them ran the whole business and no one thought anything of it. He's way out of touch with what we're capable of. Of what *you're* capable of. And that's a worry."

Josefa folded her hands into her lap and sighed. "I know, Mother. It's just . . . Well, I would like to be married before the baby comes. I don't know, it'd just feel better somehow."

"And are you sure Leo will treat this baby as his own, truly accept him or her? Have you discussed that side of it?"

Josefa screwed up her face. "Not really. And from what he said about Rory the other day — well, you know he doesn't rate men who haven't 'made it' in the world, who aren't wealthy or in the professions. He's horrible about Santiago as well. Truth is, he probably underestimates Caleb for exactly the same reason. And that would be a big mistake."

Valentina tested the weight of the coffee pot. "More coffee, darling? It's lovely to have this time together to talk without the house getting in the way. Let's hope we can do this more in the future."

She leaned over and refilled Josefa's cup. "Speaking of Santiago, you know he's given notice? He's going to work for Antal."

"Notice? No! When did this happen?"

"It's not official yet, so don't say anything. He's finishing up a few things for Caleb before he goes. I think they discussed it at the christening. He feels he's got to move on. Take steps to secure his future." She reached out her hand to take Josefa's wrist. "Are you all right dear? You look rather pale."

Josefa peered down at her cup, but her vision was blurred. Her eyes were wet. She felt for the handle. Santiago was leaving? He couldn't leave. He was always there . . . Just like Caleb's deerhounds, Venus and Jupiter, were always there. For whenever you needed a friend.

She felt a tiny fluttery kick in her stomach. Was that? Yes. Yes. Her baby. When her baby was born, Santiago wouldn't be there to hold it. To be a kind uncle. The baby had chosen this moment to remind her that he or she would be there, but Santiago wouldn't.

She jerked down her cup and rested her hand on her rounding belly. "I'm feeling strange. I think the baby just kicked for the first time."

She raised her eyes to Valentina's expectant face. "Santiago can't leave! He's part of the family. Oh, this is all so wrong."

9

Josefa slept badly and rose early, planning on taking an early morning ride. She figured if she took it gently, she could ride for a few more weeks before she became too rotund. As she strode to the stables to saddle up, she tried to banish the wisps of dream that hung in her head from last night.

She'd been standing on an open plain, gazing at her mare Esmeralda. The horse was normally so biddable, but in her dream, she shied and wheeled and refused to come to her for the sugary treat she held in her hand. A feeling of loss washed over her. Esmeralda wasn't letting her get near.

She stepped into the dimness of the stalls, and her eyes prickled with the hay dust that always danced in the air in here, filling her nostrils with its green, promising smell. She halted to rub her lids clear, and when she opened her eyes again her heart jumped. Santiago was already here, saddling up his own horse ready to ride, his back to her, seemingly unaware of her presence.

The dim light caught the sheen of his long brown hair, tied off his face at the back of his neck. He was crooning softly to the black gelding, his strong deft movements as he checked the tightness of the girth, the tension of the bridle, showing him as the consummate horseman he was.

The hay dust reached her nostrils and she sneezed. Santiago was startled by the sound. He stiffened his body, and the muscles in his jaw tightened. His hazel eyes were stony, their expression unreadable. He turned back to the horse without speaking.

"Santiago!" Her voice sounded unnaturally high and pleading. This wasn't at all like their normal casual banter, idle chat about the ranch, the horses.

He still did not speak.

"Are you going riding?"

Well, that's a clever thing to say when he's saddling up a horse.

She tried again. "Of course you are, you're saddling up Apollo. Can I come with you?"

They often rode the range together. She'd learned a lot from him as they did, random information she loved hearing. When the bulls were ready for round-up, when the nurse cows would be calving, why Caleb had chosen to breed Angus stock. Stuff Caleb never talked about with her.

But clearly Santiago wasn't in a chatty mood. His shoulders stiffened as she stepped closer.

"I don't think that's a good idea this morning." His eyes flicked to the stall where Esmeralda stood, already expectantly hanging her chestnut head over the rail, looking to Josefa. "I'm in a hurry."

He patted Apollo's saddle, as if confirming the final check that he was ready to mount.

He raised a foot to the stirrup, and hesitated. "Besides, Leo wouldn't like it."

"Leo?" Her echo of his words was tinged with a faint helplessness, and then fresh confidence surged through her. "Oh, he doesn't like to ride, so it shouldn't bother him."

"Not today, Josefa. I'm in a hurry. I've got a lot to do. Get Mariano to go with you if you want company."

He brusquely led Apollo out of the stable past her and, without another word, mounted and rode away.

10

"That's it, Mariano." Santiago looked on approvingly as the orphaned twin calves he'd brought in earlier in the day bunted the nurse cow's soft udder, their back legs splayed, heads tucked under her flank, as they happily fed. The loamy cream smell of warm milk pervaded the air.

Mariano grinned, showing his gapping front teeth. "She's taken to them like she's their real mother. She's a reliable old cow, is Daisy. It wasn't hard to mother them up."

The young calves, both female, had the glossy black coats and deep chests of their sturdy Angus bloodline. As part of the farm's valuable breeding program to improve Del Oro's beef quality, they represented another win.

Santiago clapped the ranch hand on the shoulder. "The boss will be pleased. Now go and get your dinner. We're done for the day."

He was turning to wash up and then join the rest of the men in the cook house when he heard a quiet feminine voice from a few feet away. "Santiago. Can we please talk?"

Josefa stood, one foot up on the railing penning in the calves, looking at him.

He reluctantly stepped back to the grassed lot, keeping his silence.

His heart quickened, fluttering in his rib cavity like a caged bird, a warning sign if ever he knew one.

Don't get drawn in here. She's only trouble.

She gestured towards the calves. "Looks like you've done a nice job here. Did you have to trick her to take them on?"

He shrugged. "We brought in some of the placenta, yes. The mother was already dead. Didn't look like they'd any chance to feed before she gave up the ghost." He took in the rousing sight of the pair of wiggling tails. "Looks like they're making up for it now."

"You're so good at this, you know, Santiago. Do you enjoy it?"

He shrugged. "You know I do. I don't know anything else."

There was an expectant pause. "Then why are you leaving?"

She almost whispered the inquiry, speaking so quietly that for half a minute he was unsure he'd heard her right.

"Leaving? Who said I'm leaving?" It was his first bluffing response, and as soon as the words were out, he regretted them.

Her voice rose. "Come on, Santiago. I didn't think you'd lie to me."

She gazed at him, a self-possessed set to her mouth, as if she was fully entitled to an answer, and he felt a surge of anger.

He stepped back from the pen. "I don't know what makes you think you have a right to pry into my personal life, Josefa. As of now, I am still one of your brother's employees, and I guess, by default, one of yours. When that situation changes, you'll hear about it at the same time as everyone else."

His feet were fixed to the ground as he glared.

Her face paled, her hands fell uncertainly to her sides. She took a deep breath. "Oh Santiago, I'm so sorry. I didn't want to presume—"

"Then don't," he snapped. He turned to go and wash up.

She leapt forward and grabbed him by the forearm. "Please," she said. "Don't go. Not like this. I didn't mean . . ."

He stopped, but remained facing away from the pen, intent on getting to the wash house.

"Look, I'm sorry. Mother told me. She also told me not to say anything, but of course I couldn't mind my own business." She gave a shaky little laugh. "It's all so confusing."

He turned to her then, as a tide of warmth washed over him that he knew he would never be able to give voice to.

"Josefa, you'll be fine. You've got your mother and Caleb and Rancho Del Oro behind you. You couldn't wish for better support. Antal just helped me to see I can't be a vaquero for the rest of my life. That's all."

She removed her hand from his arm. "Yes, yes. I understand." Her eyes dropped to the ground. "I just wish everything could be different."

Not as much as I do, Josefa. Not as much as I do.

11

"You were always my favorite boy. You know that, don't you Santiago?" Benecio Valaquez Carver dashed away a tear from her cheek with the back of her hand. "And that's a terrible thing to say about my own son."

Santiago had come to see his aunt in her Sonoma home because she was the first person who might be able to give him information about Leo. Who his friends were, how he liked to spend his time, that kind of stuff. Whether he was kind to his horses. *Come to think of it, does he have any horses?* Benecio should know. Leo was, after all, her son. And the sooner Santiago could satisfy Caleb's last request to him, the sooner he'd be gone from Rancho Del Oro.

He'd caught her in a mellow, reflective mood, and it was proving hard to keep her on the topic. She'd been his mother — the only one he'd known, until he left her home at the age of fifteen. He had a vague memory of happy times when he was very young, when she'd been a single maid, taking care of her younger sister's child in an extended family with wealth and resources.

It was a common occurrence in big Californio families — an out-of-wedlock child gathered up by their kin, often with support from a wet nurse, and raised in mystery, his or her origins never referred to except within a tight inner circle.

It was a very Spanish division of public and private life that he knew only too well. Within the walls of home, secrets might be whispered. But outside its walls, nothing that impugned family honor was to be divulged. It wasn't just Luisa's reputation that would be shamed, it would have been the whole family.

There were a couple of other children of around his age — Niko and Ana, orphans from the wider family who were also being fostered within the tribal bosom — so his presence wasn't remarked upon. There were *los huerfanos*, the orphan kids. And then there was him. Benecio's favorite.

It was only when Benecio married the Scotsman Gerald Carver and gave birth to their son Leo that things changed.

"I couldn't help what happened, Santiago. It was beyond my control." Benecio mopped her eyes with a white handkerchief, the skin on her cheeks bright pink and shining damp from the continued dabbing. "Gerald was within his rights. Leo was his legitimate first-born son, his heir. And you were *adulterino*, the fruit of adulterous parents. When Luisa died, that could never be remedied by her making a legitimate marriage. We were stuck with it for life."

She blew her nose and peered over the soggy linen with mournful eyes.

"You're so like your mother, Santiago. Luisa was beautiful, clever, talented. And my word, could she sing. She could have had the pick of any man she wanted. But she was a babe in the woods where men were concerned. She let herself be seduced by a man who was already promised to someone else — not that she knew that."

Santiago's senses sharpened. It had never been a secret that his mother had been an innocent, taken advantage of by an older man, but that man's name had never been spoken in his presence. As far as he knew, his birth certificate was marked "padres no conocidos" —

"parents unknown", the statement made when neither wanted their name known publicly. That was all part of the secret pact to protect the family name.

"And now you're asking about Leo. From what I saw at Francine's christening the other day Leo's making a bee line for Fergus Stewart's girl, Josefa. Is that right?" She gave a wan smile. "He never tells me anything, but you'd have to be blind not to see what he's up to — and I'm not blind yet."

Santiago leaned forward and put his hand on her sinewy arm. Benecio was trembling. "Mama, you'll be with us for many years yet, God willing. Don't get despondent."

He caught himself. *Mama.* He still called her that in intimate, private moments like this. It was one of the things Leo had particularly detested when they were younger. For him to call his Aunt Bene "Mother".

She gave him a grateful smile and patted his hand. "But I have to acknowledge it, Santiago. Finally, I have to admit. Gerald's son is not the man I'd hoped to raise." She sighed. "All those years ago, he had to be the father. That's how it worked."

Santiago patted the back of her hand soothing. "I know, Mother, I know. Don't get yourself upset."

Santiago was coming up to three when Benecio and Gerald wed, a time when children of Spanish heritage traditionally passed from the mother's to the father's domain and control.

Gerald Carver did not share the expansive family view of his Spanish relations. He made it very clear — first in subtle, and then not-so-subtle ways — that the shame of Santiago's birth was not going to be hidden under a blanket forever. Better to distance the family from him now than be embarrassed later.

Santiago had remained in the house but was banished to the farthest wing where the *niño de acogida*, the taken-in children, were housed. It was more like being at boarding school than being with his mother Benecio.

He wouldn't have minded so much if Leo hadn't taken every opportunity he could to bait and tease and humiliate him. As he grew older, he could never fathom why Leo, who had everything, still seemed to resent him, be threatened by him. It was no contest, after all. Leo was the son and heir and he was a bastard Gerald begrudged feeding and housing.

When he was fifteen, he'd more or less run away to become a vaquero.

"Don't let's talk about this now, Benecio. It's ancient history. It's no good raking it all up again. I've been making my own way for twelve years now." He squeezed her hand. "Let me order in some more coffee. And then you've got to fill me in. I admit it. I'm here with ulterior motives. Caleb wants to know what sort of man is offering for his sister. And you're the best one to tell me that."

Benecio shook her head, her eyes glittering with untold secrets. "Oh, Santiago, if you only knew."

"Knew what?"

"I've got some surprises in store for you. Because if Leo really is going to marry Josefa Stewart, I think it's time you learned a lot more about this family."

12

He echoed her words. "About the family? What do you mean?"

"Oh, Santiago. You've heard many stories of your precious mother, I know, but you've never heard as much as a whisper about your father, have you? I think it's time you did. With Gerald gone, and now your grandfather, there's hardly anyone left who knows the full story. We need to change that before I too go to meet my Maker."

Santiago felt a bolt of excitement, followed almost immediately by a stabbing fear. He hated the thought of one day losing Benecio. She was the only family he'd ever known.

He considered her, nestled into the sofa's squashy cushions, waiting expectantly for fresh coffee. The youthful energy that had been so evident for most of her life wasn't showing in her face today. Her complexion was tinged with gray, the bags under her eyes adding deep shadows to a once-perfect caramel complexion. She didn't look as if she was sleeping well.

He was about to ask after her health when heavy footsteps sounded in the tiled hall and Leo burst into the room trailed by the housekeeper flapping her hands and crying, "Perdone, senora, perdone!"

Leo ignored her, patently unwilling to observe any niceties. When he saw Santiago sitting opposite his mother he halted abruptly and the housekeeper barely avoided colliding with his back.

"What's he doing here?" He glared at Benecio. "Mother? I said, what's he doing here?"

Benecio raised her eyebrows quizzically. "And good afternoon to you too, son. It must be, what, at least six months since you were last here. Surely you can greet your old mother before launching in?"

Leo sat down next to her in an impatient whoosh, leaned over and pecked her cheek. "Sorry. I'm in a hurry. I thought you'd understand."

"What's so important that you can't observe the normal courtesies?"

Leo glared at Santiago. "It's a private matter." He blew out an impatient breath. Santiago ignored him.

"Santiago, can you get lost? I want to talk to my mother."

Benecio took hold of his arm. "Leo, please. This rudeness is completely unnecessary. Santiago and I are about to have coffee and a private discussion. He got here first. Go to the kitchen and Ana will find you something to eat. We can talk later."

Leo scowled. He stood abruptly, wheeling around to face the wall behind him, eyes alighting on the portrait of a white-bearded man in military uniform.

"What's this I hear about Grandad's will?"

Benecio's bland humor vanished. She sat very still and straight, her eyes glittering. "What about it?"

"Is it true? That he's left Aunt Lucia's share to *him*?" He tilted his head in Santiago's direction, his voice sneering.

"Why is that any concern of yours?"

Leo thrust his hands into his pockets and swiveled toward the door as if he was going to leave and then thought better of it.

"It is, isn't it? True, I mean. How could he? First Francine asks him to be godfather of the first grandchild of our generation. Now this. It's as good as announcing to the world that the Carver family doesn't care about family honor.

"Here I am, working my fingers to the bone to get a partnership in one of the best law firms in San Francisco. Headed by a man whose wife sees herself as the guardian of public morals. Do you think they're going to take on a partner whose family rewards bastards? That spits in the face of all respectability, legitimacy, rectitude, decorum, correctness . . ." Leo's face reddened as he raved. Dots of spittle flecked his tidy sandy mustache.

"All right, Leo, we get the picture." Benecio plucked at the wool tassel on the cushion she'd pulled into her lap and let her eyes rove over Leo's agitated face. "This hasn't got anything to do with your suit for the beautiful Josefa's hand, by any chance? Have you anything to tell your old mother on that score?"

Leo bared his teeth. "What do you think, mother? How many times can we snub society's rules and still be welcome in the best drawing rooms? You of all people should get that."

13

"Well, thank goodness for that."

Benecio relaxed back into the cushions, a coffee cup and saucer perched in one hand. Ana had returned with fresh coffee and had ushered the still-fuming Leo back to the kitchen for a snack.

Aunt Bene leaned forward, her elbows on her knees, hands clasped, and fixed Santiago with one of her looks. "And you're not a bastard. I won't have you called that."

Santiago spread his hands in a placatory gesture. "It's fine. I've been called worse."

Benecio shook her head. "But it's not accurate. Californios have a special Spanish phrase for your situation, and that's *hujo natural* — a natural child of his parents. Born outside of wedlock, yes. But not a bastard. In our world once the parents of a *hujo natural* married — even if was years after the birth — everything was legitimized from that point on. Such an enlightened way to handle it. Luisa would have been distraught to hear you insulted like that, because before the Americans came that's how we viewed it."

Santiago shrugged. "I suppose from where Leo stands the only opinion that counts is Americano." He grinned. "But do go on, Aunt Bene. Now you've started, you've got to finish this story."

42

He was feeling feverishly hot one moment, shivery cold the next, and his insides quivered. He couldn't decide if he was excited at the prospect of finally learning his father's name, or terrified at what the truth might hold. Perhaps both at the same time.

"Please go on. I can't stand the suspense."

"Oh, Santiago. Where to start?" She smiled fondly at him. "Deep breath and dive in, I suppose. My two sisters, Luisa and Dominga — one older than me, one younger — were romanced by the same man. Right under our noses, in the family home, the sneak. It was easy for your father, because he was always here, doing business with the General. We all liked him. But he broke a sacred trust. No one realized he was flirting with both of my sisters, and neither of them knew about the other.

"It's what happened in those days with ambitious gringos. You know how it was, thirty, forty years ago. Take up Mexican nationality, become a Catholic, and marry a Spanish rancho's daughter. It was how men of that sort got on in the world." She sighed. "I did it myself, for all the good it did me. But staying single wouldn't have made things better for either you or me."

Santiago's palms were sweaty. "So he was courting two sisters at the same time. And what happened?"

"Luisa fell pregnant. Dominga screamed that he was promised to her. Even today, a *palabra de casamiento* — a promise of marriage — is binding. Although these days you'd probably have to have it in writing. Back then a woman could take a claim to the priest and force a man to marry her if she could prove he'd promised he would. And father wasn't going to have the scandal of one of his daughters going to a priest claiming she'd been stood up at the altar. So Dominga married the gringo."

Santiago heard nothing more.

Dominga married the gringo.

A loud rushing filled his ears. Benecio's lips were still moving, but he couldn't hear a word she was saying for the noise in his head.

Dougal Mackinnon was the gringo. Dougal. Rory's father, who'd died just last year. He thought back to when he was a little kid — five or six, maybe. Rory and Dominga would come to visit, and he and Rory would play together. But Dougal? Dougal had never accompanied them.

Dougal Mackinnon was my father?

He raised a hand, as if to ward off any more words. His fingers were tingling.

"Hold on. Wait, Benecio. Give me a minute." He took a long, measured breath. "Are you telling me that Dougal Mackinnon was my father? Rory's Dad? Have I got it right?"

Benecio nodded, holding her silence.

"The man who did his best to bankrupt the Stewarts in a bitter feud after Dominga died?"

"The very same." Benecio's brows were contracted, the tips of her mouth downturned. "He caused a lot of strife in his lifetime, did Dougal Mackinnon."

Santiago felt a big lump forming in his throat. It was practically impossible to swallow. He opened his mouth. A croak was all that came out of it. "In heaven's name." He gasped. "That means Rory was my brother." Another gasp. "Well, half-brother. And I never knew."

An avalanche of bottled-up sorrow threatened to engulf him. All the unshed tears of not knowing he'd had a little brother, never knowing when Rory was murdered so brutally just a few months ago that it was his brother who'd perished. *All the lost opportunities.*

His chest heaved. He bunched up his fists and screwed them into his eyes in a vain attempt to impose some control on himself.

And so that the baby Josefa is carrying is my nephew. Or niece.

"Benecio, I need some time alone," he gasped. "I need time to think."

He blundered out of the drawing room and into garden. The afternoon was warm and still, the bees buzzing in Benecio's roses a reassurance that the rest of the world had not turned upside down. Some things were the way they'd always been. As Santiago pitched blindly down the path, he inhaled the spicy rose aroma, and slumped onto a garden bench.

His head fell into his hands, and he allowed himself a long, relieved exhalation. He was alone, as he'd wanted. But would he ever make sense of what he'd just heard? At this moment, he doubted it.

In the foyer just inside the door leading out into the garden, Leo loitered, an excited, self-satisfied grin on his face. He just couldn't suppress it.

It was something that had gnawed away at him. All his life. Why was Santiago so special? Why did Benecio's loving glance always search him out in a room before she looked for *him*? No matter that he'd had a father — a good father — and Santiago had none. It was his mother's love he'd wanted most, and he'd always come in second in the running.

It had chewed at his guts, this desire to be rid of his rival, once and for all. To get his revenge on Santiago, even if he was the apple of his mother's eye.

He corrected himself. *Because* he was the apple of his mother's eye.

And now he saw exactly how to do it.

14

"Oh Leo, there you are. Did you have a nice lunch?"

One glance at her son's face told Benecio he was in a far better mood now than when he left them half an hour ago.

"Very nice. Ana's huevos motuleños were excellent, I must say." He smiled. "Love those black beans with the chili sauce and ham."

"So." Benecio hesitated, fearful of spoiling his good mood. "You wanted to talk to me?"

"I did, Mother. About this San Francisco partnership I'm going after. It's so important to me. It will set me up for life. I just can't afford to miss out."

Benecio felt a familiar heaviness wash over her. How many times had Leo come to her with demands for things he "must have right now." The boy was still in his twenties. That was young to expect to secure a partnership in a lucrative legal practice.

"Oh, Leo, I'm sure you won't miss out, ultimately. You're still young. I'm sure you'll give it a good shot, but if it doesn't happen this time, there'll always be another chance."

"No, you don't understand. I can't afford to wait."

"What do you mean you can't afford to wait? You've got a good job, you're learning lots. No one gets it all immediately."

"Mother. Listen to me. I have to get that partnership, or I'm going to go under."

The heaviness she'd felt intensified into a deadly weight on her chest. The breath rasped in her throat. Was she having an asthma attack? She consciously tried to slow the air going in and out of her lungs, while also calming her racing mind.

"Going under? I don't understand. You received a very substantial inheritance from your father just two years ago. How can you say you're in danger of going under?"

"I've had a bit of bad luck. Invested in a bad lot. I've borrowed to try and get out of it and dug myself in deeper. If I don't get my hands on some cash very soon, I'm on the rocks."

He gave her a winsome smile, his blue eyes wide and guileless.

Benecio let out a deep sigh. She recognized this Leo, with his "calculated to appeal" act. She'd watched it evolve from when he was a little boy, using it to get another cookie at eight years old. Now he was nearly twenty-eight, and hoping it will win him the big prize of what? Thousands?

"I need Grandad's inheritance money. All of it. I see no reason on earth why it shouldn't go to me rather than that … that mongrel of Lucia's. She only brought disgrace on this family and now he threatens to do the same. He should just get back in his hole."

The sunny smile had vanished, replaced by the much more familiar jealous scowl.

"Leo, it isn't mine to dispense. Your grandfather made his choices and they must be honored. Surely as a lawyer you understand that?"

"What if I were to challenge it in court?"

She gave a short sharp laugh. "I can't see you risking the bad publicity to do that. Wouldn't you just be drawing attention to a situation you want to keep hidden?"

Leo clenched his fists, and his voice rose in register. "It would have been best if they'd all died. Then I wouldn't have to put up with this."

"Leo, who are you talking about?"

"You know very well. Santiago. Dougal and Dominga."

Benecio's heart chilled, her pulse slowed.

"You've been eavesdropping." Her voice cracked. "Listening in on a conversation that was none of your business." She spat out the words with a venom she rarely felt. "Leo, I warn you. If you make any attempt to use this information to harm anyone, anyone at all, I will see to it that you live to regret it. Do I make myself clear?"

Leo's blue eyes widened at the finality of her statement. She'd never spoken to him like this ever before. His jaw remained clenched shut.

"Do you understand?"

"Why is he so important?" The bitterness spewed out with the words. "Why do you care so much? It's always been the same. It's all about Santiago."

"Leo, that's a ridiculous thing to say and you know it. From the time you were born your father always ensured you took precedence. You got the best tutors while Santiago was sent off to the orphan's wing with the foster children. From the age of ten Gerald sent him off to the brothers for most of his lessons. You know that. How can you say it's all about Santiago when it so plainly wasn't?"

"I knew you wouldn't understand."

"Leo, I'm telling you. Anything you overheard today, forget it. It's none of your concern. Do you understand? You've had more than your fair share. You'll just have to learn to live with what you've got."

Leo's mouth curled. A corded vein throbbed in his neck. "You'll live to regret this conversation, Mother. I can tell you that. One day, you'll remember this and be very sorry."

He bunched his fists at his sides and strode out.

15

"Caleb, Josefa. Come quickly. There's something you must know."

Leo had gone to his mother's in a somewhat lackadaisical mood, hinting he was making some new arrangements to do with his grandfather's will. He arrived back a day later full of drive, with a sense of mission Caleb previously hadn't seen in him.

"I have information that has a direct material impact on the well-being and understanding of your — of *our* family."

The siblings exchanged bewildered looks and Caleb gestured to an armchair in the family sitting room. "You'd better sit down. I'll get Rosario to bring in some coffee." He ducked out to let her know while Leo smirked.

"Did your visit to your mother's go well?" asked Josefa, aware her face was reddening from resorting to such a blatant "fishing" question.

"Well enough," Leo answered. "You'll certainly be shocked to hear what I learned there."

Caleb came back into the room. "Rosario will be here in a few minutes." He plopped down in a chair opposite Leo. "So, what's the cause of all the excitement?"

Leo took a few moments to compose himself. "It's a very serious matter I have to report, very serious indeed. But as Josefa's fiancé, I feel it's my obligation to alert you."

"Alert us to what?" asked Josefa. "You're sounding awfully dramatic, Leo."

"This isn't a minor matter, Josefa. It's tragic what's been going on."

"Tragic?" said Caleb. "Oh, for goodness sake, Leo, out with it."

"It's Santiago. He's a Judas in your midst. For years now, he's taken full advantage of your kindness to him while he's been plotting against you behind your backs."

The Stewart siblings stared at Leo, both too shocked to speak. Then Caleb chuckled. "That sounds like total nonsense to me, Leo. You'll have to do better than that."

Leo turned to Josefa. "Josefa, do you have any idea who Santiago's father is, or rather was?"

She shook her head.

"You Caleb? Any idea?"

"As far as I know, his father has never been identified. Even Santiago doesn't know who he is. It's personal, and it's never been relevant."

"What if I told you that his father was none other than Dougal Mackinnon, the scoundrel who's made your life hell for the last decade?"

Josefa's hand flew to her mouth. "That can't be! He'd have said something, surely."

"The fact that he didn't just makes it all the more sinister. How do you know he hasn't been plotting with the Mackinnons all along? Acting as a spy in your household? Who knows, he might even have had a hand in Rory's death. How would you know, if someone can be that deceitful?"

Caleb jumped up, pulling at his hair, so agitated that when he spoke next, he stammered. "S-s-stop it, Leo, Stop it."

He paced the length of the sofa and back and swung to face Leo. "How do you know this? On whose say so? It could all be venomous gossip."

Leo couldn't keep the triumphant edge from his voice. "I have it on my mother's best authority. She was there. She saw it all happen. And she confirms it. Dougal Mackinnon was Santiago's father."

He locked eyes with Josefa. "I am so very, very sorry Josefa. But doesn't this cast your betrothal to Rory Mackinnon in a whole new light? Isn't it likely his older brother put him up to it, just so they could get their hands on your land?"

Josefa threw an anguished look to her brother. She put her hands over her ears and pitched forward, dropping her head to her stomach, head low, staring at the floor.

"I don't want to hear any more of this, Caleb." She was half-crying, half-shouting. "Tell him to stop. Tell him to stop right now!"

16

"Is something wrong?"

It had taken him a few days in San Francisco to find what he wanted, but Santiago had returned to Del Oro overflowing with certainty that Caleb would be pleased — maybe even impressed — by how much information he'd been able to assemble on Leo in such a short time.

He'd imagined them having a good long chat about all that he'd discovered, then Caleb clapping him on the back and sending him merrily on his way. He had very little to pack and for days now he had been preparing his heart for leaving these people who were the closest thing he'd known to family. He wanted to do it with a buoyant spirit. He had a lot to be thankful for, and the General's bequest was the final cherry on top.

Well, so much for the day-dreaming. What he hadn't expected was to be greeted by the cool poker face Caleb always wore when he was faced with something unpleasant.

His head jerked up from examining the papers in front of him at Santiago's question, but he didn't answer. Instead, he gave an ominous sigh and gestured to the seat across the table from him.

"Sit down, Santiago. I suppose the sooner we get this over with, the better."

Santiago felt his brow crumple. He hadn't told Caleb anything of his findings yet, so why was his mood so down?

He took his hat off and hung it on a wall hook before sitting down. "I've got some worrying stuff to report, no doubt about that, but I'm not sure why you already seem down to it before I've even said a word. What's up, Caleb?"

Caleb pitched his hands in a steeple in front of his mouth, his elbows resting on the tabletop in front of him. "Well, just one thing, I suppose."

He contemplated Santiago over the apex of his fingers. Eyes that were usually twinkling and mischievous were flat and somber. "When were you going to tell us you're Rory's brother?"

Santiago's hands turned to ice. He gaped, looking around, as if trying to reassure himself he was in the right place. "When was I *what*?"

The hallway door was thrust open as if blasted by a gale force wind, and Josefa stood in the entry, her dark eyes stormy and accusing.

Caleb gave a quick glance her way and then picked up where he'd left off. "You heard me the first time. When were you going to admit that Dougal Mackinnon was your father? And how much inside information have you been feeding him over the years?"

A galvanizing force like a red-hot lava flow rose from within Santiago, replacing the ice in his veins. He was aware of his jaw dropping wide open, but he couldn't seem to close it. He jolted forward, bent over, his hands gripping the table edge for support. He stayed like that, bringing himself under control, testing the strength of his knees, before he pushed himself upright. Slowly, calmly, judging the distances in the room as he might the threat of an angry bull. His eyes lifted to the hallway, where Josefa remained deathly still, as if a pillar of salt.

He stared from brother to sister for one very long breath. Then he reached for the hook on the wall and wrested free the hat he'd deposited there a minute ago. His eyes bored into Caleb.

"I have spent the last few days gathering information that I imagined would be of very great interest to the patrón of a house like this. Information you begged me for. Information that I believe could help guide some very grave decisions." He cast a furious look in Josefa's direction, not caring now if she guessed he'd been spying on Leo. "I suspect, however, you're not ready to receive it. Indeed, you appear to no longer require it. You've already made your minds up about what you think you know. Well, far be it from me to shatter your illusions." He smashed his hat onto his head and bowed. "I'll collect my things and be gone."

He turned towards the front door, that heavy, leather-paneled oak door that had been like a welcome home sign to him for a long time now. *This may be the last time I'll ever walk through it.*

Another thought came to him in the red mist that still filled his head, although his words were flowing crystal sharp. "One other thing. Thanks for not bothering to check with me first."

He started for the door and whirled back once more, as yet another thought struck.

"Caleb, good luck with your brother-in-law-to be, Señor Carver. I'd watch he doesn't cut you up into little . . ." He drawled out the word into a caricature of itself. "Lee-t-le." He brought his right hand up, his thumb and forefinger measuring out a very small distance. Then he closed the gap between his thumb and forefinger more tightly. "Very lee-t-le pieces."

17

Santiago strode out to his accommodation hut feeling as though he had a fire at his back, but once he'd shut and locked the door his arms drooped to his sides and his knees turned to liquid. Collapsing onto his bed, he lay on his back and soaked up the calmness of the tiny space. The only sounds were the occasional whistle that drifted on the breeze from one of the boys on the open range, and the isolated cry of prairie birds hunting for food.

Eyelids half closed, his energy depleted from the surge of emotion he'd just expended, he slid his view around his room which had been home since he'd been promoted from the bunkhouse several years ago. It was spartan, the wall decorated with nothing but a calendar pinned with his own notations scrawled on it. "Calving starts." "Spring round-up." "Put out the bulls."

He let out a long sigh. This world was no longer his world. He moved his hands from his sides to behind his head and took stock.

He was Santiago Valaquez Mackinnon. Santiago: the old Spanish form of "Saint James," and he knew he was no saint. Valaquez: from his mother. Despite her fall from grace, Lucia came from noble blood and he could be proud of her. *Mackinnon.* He wasn't sure he'd ever want to use that name, but it completed him somehow. At least now he could choose to apply it if he wished. Dougal Mackinnon was no saint either, but not so bad until he fell under Consuela's thrall, an old man with a voracious young wife, too weak to stand up to her manipulations.

He suddenly thought of his schooling with the Brothers, and stories of Herod the King, shamed into ordering the execution of John the Baptist to satisfy his stepdaughter Salome after he was carried away by her erotic dance.

Dougal Mackinnon was a faint version of Herod Antipas. For much the same reasons — wanting to please his wife, and playing up to a pretty young thing, he'd acquiesced to pursuing Fergus Stewart with vexatious legal claims he knew weren't valid. It was probably the same fatal weakness that got him in trouble with the Valaquez sisters, Santiago mused.

The man who fathered him was no great role model, but it was such a relief to simply be able to name a father! It completed him in ways he'd never have imagined. It was like the pieces of one of the jigsaw puzzles Benecio loved finally coming together.

He'd resisted the temptation to search. All these years he'd told himself it didn't matter if he didn't know his father — but now, he saw, it did. *I feel more like myself than I can ever remember. Does that even make sense?* He stretched out on the hard, narrow bed with the horse-hair mattress that fitted every crick and crack of his body and slipped off into an irresistible dream.

Santiago Valaquez Mackinnon. Master of his own destiny. A husband and father. A *loving, responsible* husband and father. A man capable of doing a good day's work and being paid well for his labors. He felt the mantle descend, swirl around him; he could almost swear he could feel its whisper on his skin.

A man who could stand on a mountain top and own it.

He grinned.

Santiago, you are talking a lot of nonsense. Good job you're the only one who can hear it.

But somewhere deep down inside he knew it was more than a fantasy. He could stand on a mountain top now, and he'd never felt he had the right to do that before.

He felt a flash of anger at that scene with Caleb and Josefa. They hadn't even given him a chance to give his side of the story. Well, that was going to be their loss.

He'd always stood in someone else's shadow, found guilty before he'd drawn his first breath, always been self-effacing, unassuming. Those days were over. He'd left that world behind, and he was never going back.

18

He woke to see the sun slanting through a window high in the outside wall. For a moment he wasn't even sure where he was, and then it came flooding back. He was still at Del Oro, in his hut out the back. Must be about 4.30 in the afternoon, he guessed.

Too late to leave for Orleans Hill today, but he was glad to have a chance to stay longer and hopefully thank Doña Valentina for everything she'd done for him before he left. Maybe try and explain it all to her if, unlike her children, she was willing to listen. He'd like to do that.

There was a heavy knock at his door, and he realized that had been what had roused him.

A thin voice came through from outside. "Señor, it's Mariano. You're wanted, Señor."

Mariano. What on earth did he want?

He slid off the bed and crossed to unlock and open the door.

Mariano stood outside, his face screwed up in an apology. "I'm sorry, Mr. Santiago. I really am. But Miss Josefa, the señorita, she wishes to speak to you. She asked me if I could come and get you."

Santiago scowled. "What's so urgent that I'm needed, Mariano? I know you've got everything running smoothly. So what's the problem?"

Mariano shrugged. "She's over by the calf enclosure. She asked me to stay nearby."

"She did? Ah well, let's go and see what she wants."

As he stepped across the yard, his sleep-fogged mind was clearing. Now that Josefa was being officially wooed — maybe by now she was even betrothed to that fellow — she had to be a lot more careful about being seen with other men, especially in an unchaperoned situation. The carefree friendship they'd had, when they could go riding or inspect animals in the yards, a vaquero and one of the mistresses of the house together in a safe working relationship, was gone.

Why couldn't she just leave it to Mariano? He knew as much if not more than anyone about the calves. Santiago hadn't even been here for the last few days. He strode across the yard, bristling with irritation.

Josefa stood by the enclosure holding the nurse cow and her mothered-up twins. Even from a distance he picked up her uncertainty. She was turned toward him, chewing on her bottom lip and frowning. As they drew near, she darted a quick smile in Mariano's direction.

"Thank you, Mariano. I won't be long. I know you're busy."

Mariano slouched under the shade of a nearby tree, leaning against the trunk and lighting a cigarette.

Santiago rubbed his face distractedly, still annoyed at having his sleep interrupted. "What is it, Josefa? Surely it's nothing so urgent that Mariano or one of the others can't handle it?"

His voice sounded scratchy, even to his own ears. He sensed rather than saw her recoil at the tone. She turned quickly back to the calf pen, but before she hid herself from view, he could see her eyes were wet with sudden tears.

His heart vaulted in his chest. He stepped closer, maintaining a safe distance but shooting a quick look her way. Her forehead was dotted with tiny drops of perspiration, and she swiped at her face with the back of her hand, as if she was feeling uncomfortable in his company. She was wearing a scarlet and green dress which fell in soft folds to mid-calf and showed off her sultry romantic beauty perfectly. *She is still slim and sensuous, baby or no baby.*

Her dark eyes gazed off into the middle distance, as if she'd found something fascinating on the horizon. Her beautiful mobile mouth was turned down at the corners. She began talking without looking at him.

"Santiago this is very difficult for me to say, given the circumstances." She shot him a look of appeal, her eyebrows raised as if in desperate need.

"I'm very sorry about what happened earlier, and you were right to be angry. I don't know what we were thinking. I don't know . . . Everything has just got so confusing." She wrung her hands. "Even more confusing than when Rory was alive."

Santiago glared at her. "I suppose it is confusing when you're not willing to listen to people. Like earlier today. You didn't give me any chance to say it, but I want you to know. I only learned of my father's identity a few days ago, from Benecio. A few days, Josefa. Before I went to San Francisco for Caleb. There have been no 'years of betrayal,' as you so nicely put it. I didn't even know Rory was my half-brother when he died, for God's sake. I don't know why that matters, but it does."

A painful tightness constricted his throat. Josefa was white-faced, clutching her arms to her chest.

"My guess is Leo eavesdropped when I was talking to Benecio — he was there the day we talked — and then came racing back here to cause trouble." His eyes bored into her. "I repeat, I did not know anything about this until a few days ago. And I'm as shocked as you are."

She dropped her hands to her sides and nervously flicked out her fingers, as if to release her anxiety. "I'm so sorry, Santiago. Thanks for clearing that up. I'll make sure to tell Caleb."

"Well, when you do, tell him this too. The thing that shocked me even more than learning who my father was, is that you both believed the worst of me without even checking first. You never even asked."

He gazed into her confused eyes, which were once again filling with tears.

"Oh, Santiago. You're right. You're so right." Her voice cracked. She suppressed a sob and with what he sensed was some iron control of her will pulled herself erect. "I should have known Leo would want to cause trouble. And I'm so sorry I fell for it." She gazed up at him, a look of appeal in her eyes. "In the circumstances, what I'm about to ask you — well, I wouldn't blame you if you never want to see me again."

She dropped her eyes, unable to meet his. "I came here to ask one last favor of you, which might seem very strange coming from someone in my position, especially after what you've just told me."

She dodged away almost as soon as their eyes met, back to staring at the far horizon. "Santiago, I need your help. I do. I want you to make that report you've been working on available to Caleb before you leave." Her voice broke again, and she drew in a deep breath. "Please. Whatever it says. It would be stupid to ignore it. He needs to know."

Watching her obvious discomfort, his annoyance melted, replaced by a tenderness which left his insides quivering. "Are you quite sure? You realize what — who — it's about?"

She nodded, looking once again back over the field. "Caleb has told me." Her voice was almost a whisper. "And I don't want to be disloyal, I truly don't. But if there are things I — we — should know. It's better to know them now, rather than later."

She spun suddenly so she was facing him, her eyes bright and earnest. "Please, Santiago. Don't hold that awful scene against us. None of us seem to be our usual selves at present."

Nor ever will be again, thought Santiago.

In that uncanny way she had of seeming to know what he was thinking the instant he thought it, she turned her gaze full on his face. "Maybe those old selves are gone for good. I'm scared they're never coming back."

He shrugged, reluctant to respond, to be drawn back under her spell. "They're never coming back, Josefa. You're going to be Mrs. Leo Carver and I'm not yet sure what I'm going to be. I just know it's not Santiago the vaquero who doesn't know who his father is. That man has gone forever." He stepped away from her, resolute to finish the business. "I'm leaving for Orleans Hill first thing. But yes, I'm happy to brief Caleb, if he wishes. Get him to send someone over for me when he's ready."

He turned and signaled to Mariano with a wave of his hand. "Thanks, Mariano. You're a good man, and those calves look in prime condition. Well done."

Without looking at Josefa again, he stalked away, his shoulders high.

19

"It's not an attractive picture, Josefa. It makes me feel even more concerned that your inheritance should be covered in a separate contract, rather than be included as communal conjugal property which Leo can use however he wants. It would give you and your baby maximum protection."

Caleb's eyes were tender, a hatch of worry lines shadowing their corners. He was older, and graver, than the brother Josefa was used to provoking to exasperation. Her heart spiked in alarm. Everything, everyone, seemed to be changing so fast.

"Just go over it again, so I've got the complete picture."

They were sitting on the sunny side of the hacienda, soaking up the late-morning sun, backs against the warm adobe wall. Josefa had sought Caleb out in the stables, keen to hear all the details of Santiago's report, and they'd settled here to talk.

"He's deeply in debt. Santiago suspects far beyond what he can meet out of the resources he has at his disposal. And he's angling for a partnership in the firm he works at." He cracked his knuckles, as if steeling himself for opposition.

"Those top firms usually expect partners to buy in. They don't just hand a share to them on a silver platter." His eyes flicked to the fields beyond the house, his expression distant.

"I hear he's got some money coming from his grandfather's estate. You know, old General Valaquez." He tapped the desk with his pencil, as if snapping back from a daydream.

"They've taken their time settling that business, but actually Josefa, I think you might also be a beneficiary there. Or rather, your child is. I gather the old General left a quarter-share to each of his four daughters, or their descendants. So Dominga's share will probably be coming to you, the mother of the old man's coming great-grandchild. That's what Santiago says Benecio told him, anyway."

Josefa laid her hand over her middle suddenly feeling protective. "Really? I didn't know. I'd never have thought . . . It's as if—" She stopped herself, uncertain how to express what she was feeling. She gave a deep sigh. "I'm realizing more than ever that I'm the guardian of Rory's line. He may not be here, but his child still needs someone to watch over him or her, don't they? I mean, it's not going to be Leo's child. It's still going to be Rory's son or daughter and Leo gets to help raise it."

"That's right," said Caleb. "And I wonder if he fully appreciates that."

Josefa got up and paced slowly in front of the bench where they'd been sitting. "It always helps me to move while I'm thinking." She grinned. "If that legacy's confirmed, that's another thing that really needs to be safeguarded as separate property. It's not even really mine. It belongs to Rory's child."

Her eyes appealed for understanding, and Caleb nodded. "Strictly speaking, that's right."

"Ah, there you are! And what's right?" Leo's handsome form loomed from the direction of the stables, his eyes squinting in the sun's glare, lips curved in an affectionate smile that revealed straight white teeth.

Josefa's insides did a jump that had nothing to do with the baby's movements.

He really is the most devastatingly good-looking man.

"Oh Leo, you've found us enjoying the sun."

Josefa sounded unusually evasive.

"Seems so. How are you, Josefa? Everything all right?"

"Yes, of course. Come and sit down." She moved along the bench to make space for him.

He shook his head. "I'm fine. So what's going on? What am I missing out on?"

Caleb hesitated, as if waiting for Josefa to speak. There was a long silence. And then they both started talking at once.

Caleb stopped first. "Sorry, Josefa. You go."

"Caleb was just explaining about your grandfather's will. I gather he left an equal share to each of his daughters."

Leo's expression darkened without warning. She faltered.

"Did . . . did you know about that?"

"About what?" His stance was rigid, his arms folded across his chest.

"That General Valaquez left an equal share to each of his daughters, whether they were dead or alive, with instructions their share was to be passed to their descendants. That means that—"

Leo broke in before she could finish the sentence. "I am fully aware of what it means."

Caleb braced his shoulders, as if expecting a counter-punch. "If it eventuates, Leo, we will need a clause to cover the child's interests." His eyes flashed in challenge. "Rory's child, that is."

"I am perfectly aware of who the father is, Caleb. I don't need reminding." Leo swiveled to face Josefa. "I think you and I need to have a good talk. In private."

Josefa went to her brother later that day, her heart set on finding some middle ground. She was incredibly lucky a man like Leo was asking her to marry him, she thought. He was handsome, educated, came from a good family, he was intelligent, he wasn't a drunkard . . .

As she stood with her hand poised to knock on Caleb's office door she hesitated. Was she talking herself into this? Surely if she was certain, she wouldn't have to be rehearsing all of the benefits of being Leo's wife in her head? She shrugged the thought aside and knocked.

"Let me get this straight." Caleb wrinkled his nose in that funny way he had when he didn't like what someone was suggesting. She was certain he had no idea he did it, but it told her plainer than words what he thought of her instructions. "You'll allow everything you own to become conjugal property, but your child's share of the Valaquez estate will be under a separate contract. Is that what you've agreed should happen?"

Her stomach felt fluttery, nervous, as she nodded her agreement. "Yes. It was a compromise. Leo was pretty upset about it, but he agreed if I let all the rest go into the 'legal conjugal community' as I gather lawyers like him call it. He was pretty upset at being reminded it's Rory's baby." She rubbed the back of her neck. "I hope he's not going to resent this child."

Caleb picked up his pen. "I'll note your wishes to Tom Halliburton and get him to draw up a new contract. I know he won't like it either, but if you're certain . . ." He let the words hang in the air. "Well, we'll get him onto it. You can start reading the banns."

A shiver ran up Josefa's body, from the soles of her feet to her neck. *Is that anticipation or doubt?*

"I'm marrying this man. You know the promise I'm about to make. 'In sickness and in health, for richer, for poorer.' I think he's right when he says I need to be whole-hearted about it. And if I can help him get the partnership he so sorely craves, well, isn't that what a good wife should do?"

Caleb's face displayed none of the joy she'd have hoped to see when she was announcing she was certain of her man.

"I just hope for both of our sakes this works out. Josefa. I'd hate to see some of Rancho Del Oro mortgaged or sold to pay for Leo's bad investments."

20

Francine and Antal Esterhazy knew how to throw the best parties, where the guests felt special but the atmosphere was still relaxed. Josefa's dress felt a little tight around the middle and she had kicked her shoes off under the table. But she couldn't deny the frisson of excitement she felt at being here. After all, this was Rory's family. If he was still here, he would no doubt be sitting next to her, instead of Leo. Though where Leo was, she wasn't quite certain. The chair to her left was empty.

She leaned to her right to speak to Caleb's fiancée Madeleine. The Frenchwoman and her brother had met four months ago and were planning to marry later this year, once the grape harvest was in. Madeleine's brother Aristide was in charge of the Oro d'Vino enterprise and had also been commissioned to be their best man, so all had agreed it would be preferable to leave the festivities till the end of the year.

"It feels strange to know I'll be married before Caleb, when he's six years older."

Madeleine dipped her head toward her to hear better and smiled. "Not just married, but a mother by the time we're wed. I'll be an aunt twice over. First Minette, and now yours. It's all so exciting."

Madeleine's face flushed. "I hope I won't be too far behind you in the motherhood stakes." They exchanged half-embarrassed laughs, and Josefa gave a satisfied sigh. It was wonderful to have a friend like Madeleine, close enough in age to understand her feelings.

A clinking of spoon against glass signaled that the host wanted their attention.

"Come on in, everyone, take your seats. Dinner is about to be served." Antal Esterhazy stood at the head of the long table, the picture of an upstanding host, his braided jacket and strong form hinting at his military record in Europe before coming to America.

"Welcome to this dinner to welcome Santiago into the Valaquez family — long overdue, but now more than ever something that deserves to be honored. The key players in his life have all graduated to eternity, so are saved from public embarrassment. It's time to acknowledge his place."

He raised his eyes to the French doors that led from the buttermilk-walled dining room out onto the tiled patio. Some of the men had gathered out there, indulging in pre-dinner brandies and cigars, and as they crowded in to take their seats, they brought with them the wet-wool smell of tobacco and the deep ringing bass of their voices.

Josefa cast an anticipatory glance up, watching for Leo. He'd been in a bad mood ever since the discussion yesterday of their marital settlement, even though he'd pretty much got his own way. She'd still not dared challenge him about his spiteful distortion of Santiago's personal information. Her insides tensed at his approach.

He slid into the seat beside her and used his index finger to rim the empty glass in front of him with a dissatisfied air. "Bloody Santiago. I hope this isn't going to go on all night. I suppose they're going through this charade to give him some credibility because he's working for Antal now." He glowered. "Where's the wine?"

"Coming up." Antal called down the table and gestured to the black-jacketed maître d' to fill the glasses that needed it. "Everyone right? Good. So, I propose a toast. To Santiago Valaquez Mackinnon. A returned son restored to his family."

Josefa peered down the table to where Santiago sat at Francine's right hand. His long brown hair was drawn back in its usual unassuming ponytail, trailing down the back of his strong neck. His mouth was half open in an embarrassed, surprised smile. But that was about as much of the old Santiago she could recognize.

Francine must have taken him in hand because he wore a snappy white shirt and smart bow tie under a beautifully cut black jacket with satin lapels. Even at a distance it was clear it was fashioned from the best superfine felted wool. Normal smart evening wear for men of Antal's class on an occasion like this, but Josefa would make a confident bet it was the first time Santiago had worn anything like it.

Francine turned to Santiago with a little elbow nudge. His chiseled, tanned face dissolved into a confident smile and when he rose, the tailored cut of his jacket displayed his powerful shoulders. He didn't spend his days behind a desk, that was plain to see.

"Friends and family. I thank you from the bottom of my heart. Francine has always been like a sister to me, and I can't adequately express my gratitude to her and Aunt Benecio for all they've done. Thank you, Francine and Antal for this dinner, and for my new work. But let's move on from me and honor the next generation. Please raise your glasses to toast young Charles Esterhazy, the first of the next wave."

A ripple of approval flowed; a few people clapped before toasting the Esterhazy heir. Josefa heard the elderly lady next to Benecio murmur, "My word, he's a catch. Anyone got their hooks in yet?"

Benecio smiled mysteriously.

Josefa's chest pinched so sharply her arm jerked to her waist. Her eyes darted to the top of the table. A vivacious blonde with pretty fizzy curls and deep blue eyes was laughing at something Santiago had said, gazing at him as though he was the only man in the room. He rested his hand lightly on her wrist and half-smiled as he spoke. The pinching intensified to a cramp.

Who is that woman?

She hadn't voiced that, had she? She didn't need to. Madeleine dipped her head toward her and half-whispered, "Her name is Charlotte Schenk. Father's a German banker. Very rich. Only daughter."

Josefa's eyes widened. "How do you know that?"

"We were introduced when we arrived." Madeleine's whisper softened even further. "I'm told Daddy is a very important client in Leo's law firm."

Josefa's eyes flicked instinctively toward Leo, but he was turned away, paying attention to someone on his left.

Madeleine regarded Josefa steadily. "You don't mind, do you?"

"No, of course not. Why should I?" Leo was twirling a spoon between thumb and forefinger, ready to start on the hot seafood chowder that had just been served.

"That looks very appetizing," Josefa said.

He scowled. "As far as I'm concerned, the sooner we can get out of here, the better."

A devilish sense of challenge rose up deep from within. "You don't want to stay to say hello to Miss Schenk?"

His eyebrows shot to his hairline. "Who told you about her?"

"Told me what about her?"

Josefa realized with a jolt she'd stepped into deep water, much deeper than she'd anticipated.

Leo's eyes flicked down the table. It was plain he was already well aware of where Miss Charlotte Schenk was sitting. And who she was sitting next to.

"They make a handsome couple, don't they? Your cousin and Miss Schenk?"

An angry growl issued from deep in his throat. "Alfred Schenk wouldn't entertain the idea of his sweet daughter marrying a bastardo. No matter how much the family might like to try and whiten his name."

21

Her dress now fitted even more snugly than it had a couple of hours before, and the little toe on her right foot pinched at being jammed back into her shoes. Nevertheless, as Josefa sat next to Leo's mother on a capacious couch, she felt an all-encompassing sense of wellbeing — as though her shoulders were draped in gossamer-weight cashmere.

She had a peculiar sensation of never wanting this feeling of love and acceptance to end. Benecio's grace was magnetic, and she was overwhelmed with appreciation for the woman who would be her mother-in-law. She almost made up for Leo's prickly personality, which must have come from his father. She pressed her lips together in a tight line to stop herself from saying a word.

The two women were seated in the small but beautifully furnished sitting room in Benecio's home on the Orleans Hill estate, just a short stroll from the main house. As a devoted daughter, Francine had ensured her mother wanted for nothing.

The meal had been lavish but not ostentatious. The seafood chowder was followed by a range of dishes placed in the center of the table for guests to serve themselves — everything from goulash to veal pie, braised oxtail to shrimp in saffron cream. All accompanied by wines from the estate. By the time Josefa had finished her dessert

— a choice between apple strudel, rum balls, and vol-au-vents with berries — her eyelids were drooping and she was tempted to find a comfortable corner to doze in, but Benecio had other plans.

As the family party broke up into genial smaller groups — the men dispersed for port and cigars, the ladies to stroll the gardens or chat in the drawing room over coffee — Benecio appeared at Josefa's side.

"You go off and enjoy a port," she said to a disgruntled Leo. "I want to have a nice little chat with my soon-to-be daughter-in-law."

She took Josefa's arm and led her down the pebble strewn path to her house. "We haven't had any chance to talk, have we, dear? And I'd very much like to know you better."

The hacienda was a smaller, pared-down version of the Orleans homestead, with arched windows down one long wall giving wide pastoral views over the vineyard. Two capacious sofas sat either side of a chunky low oak table that wouldn't have been out of place in an English castle. On it were displayed a bowl of bright yellow sunflowers and an engraved silver tray on which sat a medley of wine glasses, each one different, all of them elegant and antique.

"Make yourself at home, Josefa. Slip off your shoes if you wish. I believe in comfort ahead of convention." Benecio flashed her a sympathetic smile. "They'll bring us coffee from the big house in a few minutes. I'm very spoiled."

She sank gracefully into an armchair to Josefa's left. "Leo seemed a bit out of sorts." Her eyes raked Josefa's face, leaving the obvious question hanging. After a long silence she added: "I know what he's like. I hope he isn't being difficult."

"He does seem to be in a bit of a mood," Josefa acknowledged reluctantly. "I'm not sure why, because he and Caleb have pretty well concluded the negotiations. Father Giovanni is to read the first banns this Sunday."

Benecio gestured to the server who'd arrived with the coffee. "Here will be fine." She waited while the coffee was delivered, and the attendant bowed and left.

"I'm afraid he's always a bit out of sorts when Santiago's star is rising. It's always been the same, since they were little boys. He resents any success Santiago has, so I suppose today is not easy for him."

Josefa wasn't sure if it was the rich food she'd just consumed or her fatigue, but she became aware of a nasty crampy pain digging into her ribs. Maybe this was the explanation for his malicious lies. She took a sip of the coffee Benecio poured in the hope it would clear her fuzzy head.

"Really? I don't understand. I mean, forgive me, but doesn't Leo have all the advantages?"

Benecio's eyes sharpened. "You'd think so, wouldn't you, dear? But sometimes appearances can be deceiving."

She sighed. "I partly blame myself. Santiago was so precious to me after Lucia died. He barely left my side for the first three years of his life. Those years formed deep bonds that are with us right till this day. Whereas Leo was a very different kind of boy, and his father was involved with raising him from the day he was born, always fretting about me not spoiling his son." She shrugged. "As you'll discover, it's not easy being a mother, my dear. But if I could give you one piece of advice, it would be to never be frightened of loving your children too much. Just try not to confuse love with indulgence. I suspect Leo got too much indulgence, and not enough real love, despite my best efforts."

"It never occurred to me, Benecio." Flickering light from the fire gave the older woman's kindly face a warm glow. "It is all right if I call you that?"

Benecio darted her a happy smile. "Of course."

"Tell me more about Leo's upbringing. It might help me to understand him better."

For the next thirty minutes or so Benecio outlined the unusual circumstances surrounding the birth of two boys, delivered of two sisters within a couple of years of each other. Santiago, born to Lucia, who died in the act of giving him life. Rory, Dominga's revenge, who'd arrived a year or so later.

"Dominga had to have her man, even if it meant her sister's disgrace. And then she had to have a son to match Lucia's, even though by then our poor darling younger sister was dead. It wasn't enough to have outlived her. All her life she was terrified Dougal would acknowledge Santiago as his natural son. He would have been quite within his rights legally to leave Santiago a fifth of his estate, even if he didn't legitimize his birth, but he couldn't risk Dominga's wrath. I'm not sure she ever got over his betrayal."

Benecio fingered a cross that hung around her neck as she spoke, her voice gradually becoming softer, slower, almost as if she was reluctant to return to such a tender topic.

"Dominga was over the moon when she got pregnant, because it didn't happen instantly. She had to wait for it. And when it turned out to be a boy . . . Well, she didn't bother to hide her triumph." Benecio shifted in her chair, as if aware she was broaching a subject that resurrected painful ghosts.

"She still seemed to feel she had something to prove, even though Luisa was dead. But she'd laid her claim to Dougal, she'd insisted he was hers, and she wanted to give him a son. She couldn't stand the thought that Dougal might finally recognize Santiago. That would be her ultimate shame . . . And Rory was her answer to that."

She gave Josefa's hand a motherly pat. "So three sisters had three boys — Santiago, Rory and Leo — all within a few years, and oh, how differently their lives turned out."

"That's what I really wanted to talk to you about, my dear. I saw what happened to Santiago when I married Gerald. That little boy was doing just fine without any daddy at all. He was a sunny-natured, open hearted little fellow. But after Gerald joined us, things changed; Santiago changed. He got very quiet. He didn't smile as much. He could be in a room and you wouldn't know he was there — he withdrew into himself. Gerald made it very clear that Santiago wasn't his son. And Leo never seemed to get over the fact that I'd been Santiago's 'mother' before he came along. It broke my heart to see it, but I was powerless to do anything about it."

Benecio got up and walked to the window, as if the raking up of past heartaches had made her restless. She stood gazing out at the tranquil scene before her; the neat rows of vines, ghostly shadows in the pale lilac twilight. She slowly turned back, her hands clasped in front of her.

"I'm mentioning all this, my dear, because I don't want to see the same mistakes occur in the next generation. Thankfully, Santiago is now finding a place where he can grow into the man he is destined to be, but he shouldn't have had to wait this long to do it. I don't want to see the same thing happen to your child, whether it's a boy or a girl. I hope I cause no offense when I say that the sins of the parents should not be visited on their children. Wouldn't you agree?"

It was all Josefa could do to nod. The direction the conversation had taken left her speechless.

"It's all so delicate . . . But I wondered if you've been able to talk to Leo about it?"

Josefa's discomfort grew. It had not occurred to her. None of it. The circumstances of Santiago's birth . . . Well, to her he was just reliable Santiago, her brother's right-hand man, the one she could always call on when she needed help. As for Leo, and his relationship to her future child . . . She'd been too busy trying to work out what he'd be like as a husband. She had hardly given a thought to his suitability as a father.

"Well, no. Sorry, you've caught me off guard. To be honest, I was still trying to work out how we'd work as a couple."

"And what have you decided?"

Josefa was overwhelmed with a picture of Santiago as he sat by her side at their big Easter Sunday lunch a month or so back, still wolfing down the first-course chicken when everyone else had moved on to dessert. Of Santiago in the saddle, riding like the wind to head off a drift of bulls before they broke out. Images of his tanned, intent face mingled with the smell of the open range, of earthy-green cattle odor and salty winds. She shook her head to banish his presence. In everything he did, Santiago was a man of enormous capacity, but he never felt the need to push himself into the limelight.

"What have I decided? Well, I suppose, that a woman in my situation should be very grateful to be wooed by a man like Leo."

She adjusted her position on the couch so she was sitting at right-angles to Benecio, suddenly uncomfortable with how much of herself she was revealing. She was overcome with a sudden shyness.

"He has been difficult sometimes, and I don't exactly get the feeling I'm his one and only — if there is such a thing. But I've decided to give him the benefit of the doubt. To stand by the vows I am about to make, come hell or high water."

The words had come rushing out, as she was overtaken by an irresistible urge to be honest to herself and this woman who she sensed would stand by her till death.

And with the words came a fresh strength, a renewed clarity, warring with an underlying sense of heaviness she did her best to ignore. Emboldened by her frankness, she lifted her eyes to Benecio's.

Leo's mother's face was careworn but lit by a bright smile, a strangely fond curve to her lips. "Oh, my dear. You remind me so much of myself at your age."

And then Josefa saw that her cheeks were wet with tears. They coursed down her deeply lined face and left a shimmering trace on her black taffeta gown.

"Benecio! Are you all right? What's wrong?"

Benecio shook her head, too choked for words. She sat for a few minutes, her hands tightly laced together. Then she took a heaving breath. "What's wrong? Oh, my dear, where do I begin. I just hope it takes you many years to find out."

Josefa opened her mouth to speak, but before she could get a word out the attendant who had brought the coffee bustled in. "Mrs. Carver, sorry to interrupt, but you're wanted over at the big house."

Benecio raised her eyes in surprise. "What's happened, Christoff? Is something wrong?"

"No, madam, I don't believe so. But there's an unexpected visitor, and Mrs. Esterhazy says he wants to see you."

Benecio hesitated but then wearily began to rise, mopping her eyes delicately before she left the room. "Josefa, come with me. I've no idea who this is, but I'm sure they won't mind you accompanying me. I'm enjoying your company too much to let you go."

She gave an apologetic grin and took Josefa's proffered arm. "Come on girl, let's see what this is all about."

22

Mr. Alfred Schenk had the same brilliant blue eyes as his daughter Charlotte, but there the resemblance ended. A white walrus mustache drooped down healthy ruddy cheeks either side of his firm mouth. The bright, intelligent eyes were overhung by an equally luxuriant crop of white hair that curled around his ears.

He stood in the foyer of Francine's home, leaning on a silver cane, radiating physical and intellectual power, a short chunky man in an expensive gray suit decorated with a silver watch chain.

Hovering at Benecio's side, Josefa knew even before he spoke that she was in the presence of a man used to unquestionably directing his world, rather than being directed by it.

Francine stood at his side, running her hands through her hair with a distracted air as if she hadn't quite caught up with the import of the visitor's arrival. "Mother, Mr. Schenk says he's here to see you." She screwed up her eyes, as if trying to clear confusion. "He says it's about your son."

Benecio stepped forward on what Josefa could only describe as a gust of determined confidence which quenched Francine's bemusement.

"Mr. Schenk, lovely to see you again. We have so enjoyed having

Charlotte with us today. Do come and sit down. Francine, shall we use the small sitting room?" She gestured to the room off the hallway where Josefa had seen Francine feeding baby Charlie on the day of the christening.

"Oh yes, Mother. That would be ideal." She ushered the small group forward, Benecio advancing with Alfred Schenk, Josefa and Francine falling in behind.

"Now, Mr. Schenk. Do enlighten us. My son, you say? I do hope it's nothing serious."

Alfred Schenk had rested his cane on the arm of the chair as he sat down, and now he curled his hands around his middle, as if uncharacteristically unsure of how to begin.

"It is a rather delicate matter, Mrs. Carver. But you will understand that any young man who shows an interest in my daughter — well, I make it my business to check him out. And I'm disturbed to find the young man who's been paying Charlotte attention recently is — how shall I say it? — is compromised. Seriously compromised. I wish to request that he withdraw his attentions forthwith."

Schenk's blue eyes glittered. His voice had taken on a waspish tone. "I won't have my daughter's affections put in jeopardy by . . . by, well, I am sorry to say it, but by a gold-seeker."

Josefa's lungs emptied of air, and it took all her self-control to suppress a gasp. The behavior Schenk described was so uncharacteristic of Santiago.

"Oh my goodness." Benecio's complexion paled. "Of course we regret anyone in the family causing you concern."

She inclined her head to Francine. "Francine, could you ask Christoff to seek out Santiago and ask him to join us?"

Within minutes Santiago appeared, shoulders erect, eyes clear and searching. "You wanted to see me, Aunt Benecio?"

"Yes. I want to introduce Charlotte's father, Mr. Alfred Schenk. Mr. Schenk, Santiago Valaquez."

Schenk's brow furrowed. "There's been some mistake."

Santiago had stepped closer to shake hands with the older man without requiring him to rise. Schenk grasped his hand warmly. "Glad to meet you, Mr. Valaquez. I've heard a bit about you. Glad to hear Antal's taken you on. From what I understand you're an upstanding fellow, a hard worker, with a good future."

He locked his gaze on Benecio, whose face was flushing bright pink.

"No, it's not Mr. Valaquez who concerns me. It's the other one, Leo. Leo Carver. He's a bankrupt who's been unscrupulously charming my daughter, and it's got to stop."

23

The ladies' sitting room was beginning to feel over-crowded. Extra chairs had been brought in while the ever-reliable Christoff was dispatched to find Leo, and after a small delay had returned not just with Leo, but with Charlotte also in tow. It appeared they had been "chatting" in the conservatory. Charlotte's blonde curls appeared more tousled than they had a lunch, and her complexion was distinctly pinker than earlier.

Leo, however, was his confident, urbane self, the rising star about to become the youngest partner in San Francisco. He pumped Alfred Schenk's hand, apparently unaware of what awaited him.

"Mr. Schenk! How can I be of assistance? I trust the firm is meeting its obligations to you? If not, just say, and I'll ensure it does." Leo glanced around the room, as if expecting congratulations for hobnobbing with King Croesus.

Benecio fixed Leo with an electric gaze; Santiago was staring out the window, maybe wanting to avoid Leo's attention. Most of the others in the room, including Charlotte, were staring at Leo with confused expressions.

Josefa was a mess of contradictory emotion: fury at her intended's duplicity, and a cringing anticipation for what was coming next. Leo was going to be humiliated — and, by association, she would be too.

All of her and Caleb's heart-searching, all the arguing, the negotiating, all was wasted effort, because Leo was a conman. She had fire in her veins as she wrestled with the extent of his lies. He'd faked an attraction to her just to get hold of her money.

She realized Alfred Schenk was talking.

"It's not the firm I'm concerned about Carver. I'm afraid it's you."

"Me?" Leo's eyes darted around the room, apparently finding nowhere to alight. He returned then Schenk, challenge in his voice. "What am I supposed to have I done?"

"Well, I suppose I could start with making false representations. You're presenting yourself around town as a fine, upstanding young man when you're about to tip into financial ruin. You've accumulated bad debts all over town and you owe one of our lending funds so much that if you default you could take the whole bank down with you."

The stunned silence was broken nervous shuffles. Josefa was numb. From the sudden quiet, she guessed the rest of the family were in shock. Except for Santiago. He was still gazing out the window. It wasn't clear if he was even listening. But then most of this information was probably of no surprise to him.

Schenk glared at Leo. "There's more, but is that enough to start with? And while you've been digging yourself into this hole, you've been promising my daughter the earth."

Leo darted a guilty look at Josefa and began to make a feeble protest.

Schenk raised his hand. "No. Don't bother. Charlotte's been telling her mother all about it." He shot his daughter a fond smile. "Luckily for us, she's not a dissembler." He gestured to Charlotte to come and sit with him, and she perched on the arm of his chair, her arm around her father's neck.

"We've nipped this in the bud, Carver, before you did too much damage. Charlotte's reputation is intact. And that is how it will remain. I'm sorry you have got yourself into this nasty mess, but it won't be Schenk funds that bail you out of it."

He slipped forward on his chair, placed his left hand on his cane, and pushed himself upright, slipping his right hand around Charlotte's waist as he stood. "My apologies for interrupting your family gathering, Mrs. Carver. We'll leave you to get on with it."

Charlotte shot Francine a droll look. "See you soon, Francine."

Francine returned the half-whispered farewell with a wry grin. "Looking forward to it!"

24

"Charlotte was far from heart-broken. That's just about the only good thing about it. I don't think she was too upset."

Josefa searched Madeleine's face for some sort of affirmation. Her mind was racing, searching for answers, and Madeleine was the best person she knew on whom to test out her thinking. Her stomach was still fluttering from what just taken place — and the anxious flickering had nothing to do with her baby. Her fiancé, so-called, had just been unmasked as the gold-digger he was, in front of everyone.

Father Giovanni was supposed to be reading the banns this Sunday. Did "chasing after other women" count as due cause for why a marriage should not proceed?

She came back from her ramblings with a jolt as Madeleine spoke. "You're quite right, Josefa. That young woman struck me as having a few brains, like her father. I don't think she was in the least heart-broken."

She leaned in to smell some of the lilac that arched over the Orleans garden path. They'd embarked on a quiet private stroll around the estate, stretching their legs and taking in some fresh air in preparation for the long drive home, as well as snatching a bit of private time.

"More than can be said for me," said Josefa with a self-conscious grin. "Well, maybe not heart-broken. Publicly humiliated, more like it. What was I thinking?"

Madeleine draped her arm consolingly around Josefa's shoulders. "Don't blame yourself. Leo was pretty irresistible. Good-looking, a rising star of his profession, romantic when he wanted to be . . . I can understand the attraction."

"Mmm. And very able to spot a desperate woman. The thing I found most embarrassing was that I sat in that room, his fiancée, and no one acknowledged I was there. The one who'd maybe been most wronged, when you think about it. Worse still, I don't know whether to be offended or relieved."

She stopped in her tracks and gave a disbelieving laugh. "Isn't that crazy?"

Madeleine laughed with her, and then got serious again. "Not crazy, dear Josefa. You had to at least test out the possibility of that marriage, I can see that. But you've had a lucky escape, n'est-ce pas? Where are things with Leo right now?"

"Nowhere. I haven't seen him since that mess in the sitting room. I don't even know where he's gone."

"And how do you feel about that?"

Josefa shrugged. "Hard to say. I'm pretty confused."

"But you won't be taking him back? Am I right in that?"

"Oh, you are so right. Better to remain single than feel I was his bail-out in a very expensive card game."

She sank down on a concrete bench under a tree and patted the space beside her. "Benecio had some very interesting things to say before everything blew up. I should have taken it as a warning."

"What kind of warning?"

"Oh, you know. About refusing to acknowledge things that are staring you in the face because you want to believe something else so badly." She sighed. "She told me a lot about their childhood. Leo's and Santiago's. I guess it explained a lot."

She sensed Madeleine's interest sharpen.

"So tell me. What did it explain?"

"Well, about why they are like they are. It's pretty obvious Leo hates Santiago. And I'd guess the feeling is mutual, although Santiago isn't as obvious about it."

"You'd think Santiago had nothing to rival Leo's position, so what's the problem?"

"Apparently there's a life-long jealousy there because Santiago was Benecio's darling baby boy until she married and had Leo. You'd think Santiago would be jealous of Leo, but apparently it was the other way around. Leo has always felt he's second-best to Santiago in his mother's affection. So even though he's had everything — as well as the full-on-father — he still resents Santiago's very existence."

"All very interesting, but how does it matter now?"

"Benecio was making the point that in an ideal world, whoever I marry should be willing to accept this baby of mine as his own. Her husband could never do that for Santiago, and that was a big part of the problem."

"Oh. And do you reckon Leo would accept your child?"

"When I think about it? No. Especially when I recall how he treats Santiago."

"Seems to me you're pretty close to making a decision then."

Madeleine took her friend's hand. "Forgive me if this is too personal. But have you ever considered Santiago?"

"Santiago? What for?"

"You know very well what for, you minx. I can see it in your rosy cheeks. Tell me you haven't thought of him that way, and I won't believe you."

Josefa's confusing stomach butterflies fluttered stronger than ever.

"Santiago? He's like family. That would be too loco. Like kissing your brother."

"Charlotte Schenk didn't seem to have any objections. In fact I suspect she's consoling herself for her so-called 'loss' of Leo with thoughts of Santiago even as we speak."

Somewhere deep down Josefa's chest pinched at the suggestion.

Madeleine was watching her face closely. "Yes! You don't like the idea of that too much, do you? I see it."

Josefa had been picking apart a lilac blossom, savoring the sweet fragrance on her fingers, and she now picked up the crumpled bloom and threw it playfully at Madeleine.

"Shut up, you French provocateur. Caleb knows you're trouble, doesn't he? Or rather, he's *in* trouble?"

The laughter they shared successfully deflected Madeleine's questions. But it couldn't erase the picture of Santiago in her mind, his fluid bearing, the aura he had of a slow, deep river occasionally lit by a quicksilver mischievous smile, like the sun on smooth water. A rolling sense of the peace and safety she experienced whenever they were close enveloped her, and then just as quickly vanished again.

"Santiago's got his new life now," she said. "I don't think he's looking backwards."

"Josefa, Leo might be part of the reason he moved on. And yes, he does have a new life. Finally having his parentage properly recognized and, I gather, inheriting some of his grandfather's estate — well, I suspect they'll have put some missing pieces in place. But you'd be a fool to ignore him."

25

"Leo!" Josefa's tone was peremptory. "Where are you going?"

His boots crunched on the gravel path as he tossed a response across his shoulder. "Where do you think? I'm leaving."

Josefa shivered and drew her shoulder wrap up around her neck, warding off the sharp evening chill. She was standing just outside Francine's front door. A dozen yards away was a cab, clearly waiting for a new passenger.

"Without saying goodbye to me? Without any explanation? Don't I deserve better than that?"

Leo's stride slowed. He'd been heading at a determined clip for the cab. His face when he turned towards her was flushed, but his eyes blazed in defiance.

"Do you think I enjoyed being humiliated like that in there? In front of everyone? I've got to get back to town and shore up my reputation before I'm completely destroyed."

He stamped his feet in protest. "After Schenk's little display I'll be lucky to have a job. You can forget about the partnership."

Josefa stepped right up to him and stared into his eyes. Toe to toe, she felt a frisson of power, instantly gratified to be nearly as tall as he was.

"And where does that leave me? What has this whole exercise been about, Leo? You were the one who came on strong, not the other way round. And so now you're walking away without a word?"

"Josefa, you're a beautiful woman, but let's be honest. It was never going to work—"

"Oh really? And why is that?" Angry heat was flushing through her, carrying away with it any feelings of rejection or loss. *How dare this cocksure cur discount me.*

The defiance in his eyes faded, replaced by a dull, defeated glaze. "Josefa, let's face it. When I was at the top, I could afford to take on damaged goods." His eyes slid to the ground, unable to meet hers. "Especially with the settlement you brought with you, it was worth the risk. But now — well, I can't afford any questions about my social status. I'm going to have to do a lot of repairing to regain my place in le monde. I can't afford to make a controversial marriage. Not now."

He darted her a quick hangdog look. "Sorry." He flashed a longing grimace towards the cab. "When your brother hears about what went on in there, he won't agree to the match anyway."

"I'm of age, so I don't need his consent. But it was always about the endowment, wasn't it?"

He shrugged. "You can't do much without it."

"There are things that count for more, Leo. Like being true to those you make an undertaking to. Like being a good father."

She, too, gazed down the drive to where the cab driver patiently waited, lamp in hand.

"I should thank you." She didn't take her eyes off the cab driver, who was shuffling his feet restlessly. "You've helped me see what really counts, at least as far as I'm concerned. I guess we've both had a lucky escape."

26

She had just one regret about not marrying Leo, Josefa admitted, as she curled her stockinged feet under her and snuggled into the fur rug on Benecio's couch. And that was missing out on having Benecio as her mother-in-law. The woman was pure gold.

She leaned forward to catch the heat from pine logs roaring in the stone-faced fireplace and stared into the dancing flame, mesmerized by the sparks flying up the chimney. The pine-smoke smell reminded her of Christmas. Doña Valentina was a wonderful mother, but she didn't have the gift for nurturing that her cousin did. Benecio's home was one place in the world where Josefa felt unconditional acceptance. Undeserved love. She wondered once again how Leo could have grown into such a dissatisfied man under such tender care.

"Here we are my dear. A hot chocolate to brighten the spirit." Benecio's comfortable, maternal form bustled into the sitting room with a tray carrying two steaming cups in hand.

It had been ten days since Josefa's public humiliation by Alfred Schenk, and she had been secluded at home at Rancho Del Oro until today.

Her waistline was still expanding, and she felt increasingly self-conscious about being seen in public. However, even more than her expanding middle, her cheeks flamed at her recollection of that scene at Francine's. She'd maintained a bold face when she parted with Leo. She didn't want the man any longer, she was certain of that. She wasn't sure she ever had wanted him, if she was honest with herself.

But it still stung to have learned about his divided attentions along with half the family, in such a public way. His dalliance with Charlotte Schenk — if it could even be called that — occurred before he took up with her, that seemed clear. But Alfred Schenk's shaming of him as a suitor for his daughter couldn't help but reflect on her. Was she the one left with the Schenk reject? And from what he said, it sounded as if Leo's financial problems were even worse than Santiago had been able to discover.

"You're not still brooding over Leo, are you dear?"

Benecio sank into the armchair to Josefa's left and passed her a warmed cup. Josefa's fingers curved around it, savoring the luxurious aroma of dark chocolate.

"Do you want to talk about it?"

She'd accepted Benecio's invitation to come and stay for a few days without a second thought. She was bored at home, especially now she couldn't readily go riding and Santiago wasn't around to annoy. She told herself that more than anyone, Benecio understood what she was going through.

"I don't know what there is to talk about really, Benecio. I guess Mr. Schenk's little scene made it impossible to proceed, but even if that hadn't have happened, I'm not sure we'd have got to the altar." The hot chocolate warmed the back of her throat and slid down in a soothing velvety trickle. "Mmm this is good," she said, sending an appreciative smile Benecio's way. "You do spoil me."

"You deserve spoiling." The older woman gave a little laugh. "So it sounds like you were having second thoughts about Leo? Even before Mr. Schenk spoke, I mean."

"It was what you said, really, about not repeating Santiago's story. The importance of giving my child a father who would accept him and love him or her. When I thought about it, I realized Leo was not that man. It sounds like he is more like his own father."

She scrunched up her face in an apologetic grimace. "And I decided you were right. I didn't want that. Mr. Schenk just made it easier for me to slip off the hook."

Benecio nodded approvingly. "You're a wise young woman, Josefa. Everything will work out for you. It might be a little rocky in the middle, but you'll be fine in the end."

A light tap on the door jamb caused them both to turn to the entryway. Santiago stood with his arm raised, his trademark hair scooped off his face and into a ponytail secured at the base of his neck. Whenever she saw him, Josefa thought of creative fire. He had a vitality, an individuality, that was unlike anyone else. *He should be a flamenco guitarist or Botticelli angel. When God made him, he broke the mold.*

Benecio beamed like a lighthouse on full power. "Why, Santiago, come in! Join us for *un chocolate.* Josefa's just been keeping an old lady company."

He hung back, but Benecio gestured him forward impatiently. "Come on, boy. I've hardly seen you since you started with Antal. We want to hear all about it. How's it going?"

He stepped forward and hugged his aunt warmly, acknowledged Josefa with the briefest nod, and proceeded to regale Benecio with stories of his new job.

Their talk was warm and informal, the interaction so naturally affectionate that Josefa nestled into her warm perch on the comfy sofa with the snuggly rug, and relaxed into watching Benecio and Santiago together. She got a momentary glimpse of how easy it would have been for Leo to feel left out. She even felt a momentary pang of sympathy as she thought of the small boy desperately seeking his mother's attention.

Finally they ran out of talk, and all three stared into the fire in companionable silence for a few moments. "It's good to hear things are going so well, Santiago. It sounds like it's working out very happily here," Josefa said.

Santiago inclined his head toward her, the ease he'd shown with Benecio replaced by an awkward stiffness.

"It is, Josefa. Very well. Thank you."

Benecio insisted that Santiago stay for supper, though it seemed to Josefa he was reluctant about being there. The conversation over their meal — a delicious sweetcorn soup accompanied with quesadillas, cheese-filled tortillas — relied heavily on Benecio's cheerful interjections.

With the meal over, Josefa was waiting for the perfect moment to politely excuse herself when Benecio beat her to it. With a mischievous glint the matron stood, masked a theatrical yawn with one hand and announced it was time for *la dama de la casa* to sleep.

"You youngsters can chat on. I'm calling it a day."

"Actually I'm pretty tired too," Josefa said, jumping to her feet. "I'm ready to turn in."

"No, no, finish the coffee. There's enough left for another cup each." Benecio blew them each a kiss and backed out before Josefa could protest further.

"Que pasa? What's she playing at?" Josefa hunched forward on the edge of the sofa, elbows on knees, hand cupping her chin. She locked eyes with Santiago across the distance of the sturdy coffee table.

He shrugged. "She gets a bee in her bonnet about some things."

She dropped her hand from her chin and instead leaned back against the sofa. "Things like what?"

He grinned helplessly, a ghost of the old Santiago appearing. "I don't know. Things she thinks she knows best about. Most things." A mischievous grin quirked up his lips.

Josefa gave a soft snickering laugh. "In my experience she probably does know best on most things."

"How come?" Santiago's voice was quiet, but inflected up, sounding interested.

"Oh, she just told me some things about your and Leo's childhoods when I was here last. She gave me a lot to think about." She gazed into the fire for a moment, lost in her reflections. "I came to the conclusion she was right."

Santiago shifted his long legs, as if uncomfortable. "So where are you and Leo up to? Got the date confirmed yet?" Two spots of high color on his cheekbones were the only hint the question was anything other than a casual, throwaway inquiry.

"I could ask you much the same thing. How are you getting on with beautiful blonde Charlotte, the ready-made heiress?" As soon as the words were out, she knew they sounded far more green-eyed than she'd intended. She tried to compensate. "Not that it's any of my business. She gave him a wry smile. "The banns won't be being read this Sunday or any Sunday after it. I guess I knew the writing was on the wall from what you told us, even before Papa Schenk turned up. I tried to ignore it. But as far as he was concerned, it was all about the loot."

She suddenly had the urge to talk straight and serious. They knew one another well enough for that, and Santiago could handle it. "And there was the fatherhood thing. Benecio asked me if I thought Leo would make a good father for my little one. And I had to answer in the negative. He wouldn't."

Santiago stood, as if suddenly needing to stretch. "Much like someone else we know."

"Exactly. As your aunt pointed out."

Santiago stepped around the low table and sat carefully down on the sofa next to her, leaving a safe distance between them. He cocked his head on one side. "That baby of yours. You realize it's my niece or my nephew?" His eyes raked her face. "You did, didn't you? Now that I know the truth about my father, Rory and I are half-brothers. Had you given that much thought?"

Josefa shook her head. "Honestly? I hadn't really. I mean, since you found out about all that we haven't seen each other. I still feel terrible about that day—"

Santiago waved it away. "Forget about it."

Josefa continued, "But now you remind me again, of course you're right. It feels a bit odd, but I suppose that's because it's new. It's strange for me to think of you as Rory's half-brother. I hadn't fully taken on the next step. That you are my baby's uncle . . ." She gazed up at him, aware her face bore a puzzled half-smile. Life kept on getting more complicated.

Santiago reached out and gently took her hand, his eyes serious. "If it's a father for your child you're looking for, I'll do it."

27

"You'll what?"

Josefa couldn't believe her ears. She oscillated between a surging, wild joy and equally fierce indignation. *He what? He thinks this is all that's required?*

A flash of uncertainty crossed Santiago's beautiful face then, like a wisp of cloud chased by the wind, as quickly as it had appeared it was gone. He sat forward, as staunch as ever, a hint of a smile on his gorgeous mouth.

Madeleine's voice wafted into her mind: "You'd be a fool to ignore him."

Ignore him? Bah! The man has no idea!

"You said you wanted someone who would be a good father for your child," Santiago said. "I don't usually push myself forward, but I could be that person." He stared at the fire for a few seconds, and when his eyes met hers, they were bright with unshed tears. "I never knew I had a brother until it was too late. Rory was dead before I even knew about him. I don't know, it just seems like a way I could make it up to him. And help you too, of course."

Josefa snatched her hands away from his warm grasp. "Santiago, you're loco!"

He shrank back, frowning. "What? What did I say?"

"Oh, Santiago!" Josefa was laughing now. She couldn't help herself. "Yes, I said being a father was important, sure. But it isn't the *only* thing. And admirable as your feelings of wanting to do something for Rory's memory might be—" Once again laughter rippled out of her. What was happening to her? For months, her life had been a tragedy, and now, without any warning, it was turning into a comedy. "Let's just say it's not the most flattering offer a woman could wish for. Although of course I do appreciate your willingness to bail me out." She gave him a waspish smile. "However, I think I'll hold out for the full package. You know. The husband, as well as the father bit. Thanks for offering, though."

She gathered up her full satin skirts, taking a fleeting pleasure in the ripple of the fabric around her as she stood. "Now I think I really will go off to bed. I'm glad you're happy in your new life, Santiago. I really am. And I'll be just fine, don't you worry." She padded out in her stockinged feet.

Her distinctive vanilla and lavender perfume lingered behind her, underlying the butterscotch tang of the pine fire. Jefferson pine, its fragrance unmistakable. Like Josefa's.

Santiago inhaled deeply and asked himself what had just happened. She'd said she wanted a man who would be a good father to her child. He didn't rate himself at much, but that was something he thought he could do pretty well. So why did she treat his offer like a joke?

He ran his forefinger along the familiar calluses on his right hand as he pondered the question. Already they were changing. The familiar mark where the rancho rope cut across his right palm was fading, replaced by pruning-shear indents on finger and thumb. It happened so fast. *Everything* was changing so fast. Three months ago he wouldn't have recognized himself today.

Benecio's lawyer had indicated that his grandfather's inheritance would be in his hands within the next couple of months. He could expect title to a pretty hacienda on a productive patch of wine country neighboring the Orleans, as well as a tidy bit of capital to help get set up. His dream of becoming a man of means, able to support a family, was racing up on him faster than he'd ever imagined.

He'd hardly dared hope Josefa could be part of that. In fact, if he was honest with himself, he hadn't dared hope she'd see him as a husband. So he'd jumped at the alternative.

Let's just say it's not the most flattering offer a woman could wish for.

He cringed inside and felt the flush of red heat up his neck. What a bufflehead! He'd just insulted a proud señorita. A beautiful, proud señorita. And the only woman he'd ever loved.

28

"So you turned him down?"

Madeleine and Josefa sat over morning coffee on the Vino d'Oro terrace, enjoying some early sun. Josefa had been back from Benecio's a few days, and she was relishing the opportunity to catch up with the woman who was rapidly becoming her best friend.

Madeleine's mouth crimped with amusement, but she fought to keep her expression solemn.

"Of course I turned him down!" Josefa exploded into giggles. "Wouldn't you?"

"Well, it depends." Madeleine raised one eyebrow and gave Josefa a playful "oh là là" look.

Josefa laughed again. Madeleine's naughtiness really could be irresistible.

"Depends? Depends on what for goodness sake? The man's a saphead."

"An adorable saphead. One I suspect you're already half in love with."

Josefa rose from her chair and put her hands on her hips in indignant denial, then let them linger on her baby bump in front.

"You can't be serious!" She was still laughing, pushing away the late-night thoughts she'd had about the man: his lithe silhouette, whether on his feet or his horse; the searching way he regarded her as he talked, so earnest to be understood; the way his lips curved when he smiled . . .

"Look at it this way, Josefa. You're in the family way. What will the reaction of most men be when they consider you as a future wife?"

Josefa shrugged. "That I come with unwanted baggage?" Her jaw contracted. "Let's face it, that's what they all think."

"And our bottle-head hero?"

"Well, the opposite of that. But that's not the point," she protested. "A woman in my position wants to preserve some dignity."

"Quite right. But which do you prefer? A man who welcomes your child, or one who silently resents it?" Madeleine's eyes held a wicked twinkle.

Josefa sighed theatrically. "Okay. You've made your point."

Madeleine smiled. "Just promise me one thing."

Josefa wrinkled her nose. "Why do I have an uncomfortable suspicion you know something you're not telling me?"

Madeleine remained silent.

"Oh, very well then. What do you want me to promise?"

"That you'll give him another chance. If the occasion should ever happen to arise, you won't laugh him out of court. Will you promise me that?"

"I suppose . . . Oh, all right then." She knew she sounded grudging, but Josefa hugged the thought to herself deep down inside. Though she knew, really, that miracles didn't happen.

I mean, look at the competition. Why would anyone pick me?

29

Santiago had been closeted with her brother in Caleb's study for the past hour, and Josefa was as twitchy as if she'd disturbed a hornet's nest. He didn't live or work here any more, so what business did he have here?

The study was just off the main family room, central to the house, but with the door shut and the thick adobe walls all she could hear was the low hum of male voices.

She'd tried hard to keep herself busy somewhere in the farthest corners of the house and garden, but she found herself drawn back time and time again in the hope of catching a glimpse of him as he departed.

A week had passed since the conversation with Madeleine, a week in which she'd had no opportunity to keep her promise. Santiago hadn't come near. So much for "second chances." He plainly didn't want one.

The deep rumble of the men's voices and the occasional outbreak of laughter indicated they were getting along just fine without her. Clearly, the chill that had overtaken their friendship when Leo was here had melted. They sounded like they were as close as ever.

Bully for the boys. She rubbed her itching arms and scowled. She hated being left out.

She was just wondering whether she'd get Rosario to make coffee, and then use it as an excuse to worm her way in when there was a loud rapping at the front door. *Great. A diversion at last.* "I'll get it, Mother!"

She bobbed her way to the entryway and was amazed to see Madeleine on the threshold, her arms filled with a huge, gorgeous bunch of fresh-cut pink and double-white peonies, at least two dozen of them, the blossoms dripping with their intoxicating sweetness.

"Madeleine! What a surprise! And the flowers! They're my favorite, did you know that? They're lovely, but why? They must have cost a fortune."

She dodged the dewy blooms to greet Madeleine in French style with kisses on both cheeks and led her into the family room. "I was about to get Rosario to make coffee. We'll certainly need some now! Do sit down!"

Madeleine gestured to the flowers. "Better get Rosario to fill some vases too. Oh, just to be clear, they aren't from me." She plucked a scallop-edged ivory card from the stems and presented it to Josefa with a flourish. "You have an admirer."

Josefa couldn't remember when she'd felt so knocked off her feet. *An admirer? There must be a catch.*

She stared at Madeleine, the card arrested in her hand. "You're kidding."

Madeleine shook her head. "Read it."

Keeping hold of it, too scared to look, Josefa went to the kitchen and asked Rosario for vases and coffee. She followed the housekeeper out as she gathered up the sweet blooms, and then dropped into a chair opposite Madeleine.

"I suppose you know who it's from?"

Madeleine laughed in delight. "Just open it!"

Josefa's fingers didn't want to work. They were frozen in fearful anticipation. What if it wasn't what she hoped for?

She gingerly opened the card. Inside, it contained a folded sheet of notepaper and a simple inscription: "Cariño. My heart, My life. S."

Josefa's heart was beating so hard she thought it might jump out of her chest. She opened the note.

An hour to know you, a day to love you, but it will take me a whole life to be able to forget you.
Una vida lograr olvidarte.

"Oh, Madeleine!" Her face was wet with tears.

The door to Caleb's study opened, and her brother and Santiago stood in the threshold.

"Josefa!" Caleb's cheerful voice boomed out. "Santiago's here, and I think he has something he wants to show you."

Her eyes locked on Santiago's face, so familiar, and yet so new. He was taller, stronger, more confident than the boy she'd laughed and played with. His eyes were steady with intent. In his hands he held a large white box, tied up with a broad satin ribbon, a big bow on top.

He closed the distance between them and held the box out in front of him. Still a little dazed by the succession of unlikely events, she took it from him in an automatic reflex action. They stood, inches apart, immobilized. Then he reached his hand with infinite grace to her face and traced the line of her cheekbone with his index finger.

"My heart, my love. Mi corazón, mi amor."

A long silence followed and then he stepped back. "Open it, Josefa. What's in there speaks more eloquently than a humble vaquero ever could."

She raised her brows. "Humble vaquero," she snorted. "Rogue hombre, more like it." But she was grinning with silly delight as she said it.

She dropped back into her chair and the two men joined them at the table, quietly greeting first Madeleine, and then Rosario who returned with the flowers and the coffee. Josefa opened the gift box and began to read from an enclosed parchment sheet. About a dozen clauses were inscribed in a fine calligraphy, presented like a legal document.

Josefa's hand went to her mouth. She could barely breathe.

A contract to honor a lifetime.

I, Santiago Valaquez MacKinnon, knowing Josefa Martinez Stewart to be a woman of keen intellect and penetrating acumen, hereby offer my life, my love, and all my human strength and frailty to uphold and honor her in full happiness, as long as we both shall live.

The Pre-Marriage Contract: Presenting an unusual trousseau.

Namely, herewith: Twelve Ways Santiago Honors Josefa.

One black mantilla in the finest Spanish lace, suitable for weddings and funerals.

An engraved glass perfume bottle filled with Spanish jessamine toilet water, the favored sweet fragrance of a dark-haired beauty.

A bouquet of two and a half dozen peony blooms, wonderful to behold, but no more beautiful than the mistress of the house that others like them are destined to fill.

A certificate of transfer of the favorite mare Esmeralda, in foal, to anywhere Josefa should so desire, signed by Caleb Stewart, ranch owner.

A solitaire diamond engagement ring in a velvet box, to be worn on the lady's finger if she assents.

A carved oak chest, filled with a selection of fine linens. (Awaiting the lady's attention at the Orleans Hills estate.)

A bolt of finest gold cloth: suitable for a wedding dress.

A bolt of black silk: ditto.

A bolt of embroidered white silk: ditto.

A pretty baby's cradle fitted with linen. A nod to our future.

A commission for a portrait by a well-known California photographer. Because I never want to forget how beautiful you are today.

There was another signed certificate, from Caleb, promising Josefa one of his hound Venus's puppies, should she so desire.

Every now and then Josefa had to stop and dash away tears with the back of her hand. Even so, before she got to the end, her sight was so blurred she had to stop reading. She flashed a look at her silent, intimate audience, shuddering with joy and tenderness.

Her smile was wide and fixed. She knew it but couldn't seem to moderate it. "Santiago, I—"

He stood and gestured. "Finish it, Josefa. You need to finish it." His voice was quiet but authoritative.

She scrutinized the parchment, the sheet trembling in her hands. Right at the bottom were two signatures and a blank space for a third, jiggling around in her compromised sight.

She brought the page up and read more closely.

A Statement of Intent:

I, Santiago Mackinnon, undertake to carry out all promised in this document, as a precursor to our marriage, if Josefa Stewart so accepts.

Santiago's bold signature trailed to the edge of the page.

Witnessed and upheld by Caleb Stewart, brother and close friends of the affianced pair.

Caleb's signature followed.
And right at the bottom:

I, Josefa Stewart, accept the offer of marriage presented today by Santiago Mackinnon, and undertake to embark on the appropriate preparations and agreements to seal the nuptial contract as soon as is decently possible. Signed . . .

Josefa gazed at Santiago, who remained standing, a few feet from her, his face expectant but solemn.

Her eyes flicked to Madeleine, teasing. "What a set up! What was it you made me promise a week ago, Madeleine? That I'd give him another chance?" She turned back to Santiago, her heart so full she could barely speak. "I always knew you'd make a wonderful father, Santiago. And after today I'm satisfied you'll be a magnificent husband. *My* magnificent husband." Tears spilled down her cheeks again. "Oh, for goodness sake, someone give me a pen before I turn this whole thing into a soggy mess."

With courtly ceremony her brother unscrewed the top of a bottle of black ink and dipped in a nibbed pen. "Here you are. Get it over with. And thank goodness you two have finally seen the light."

30

The thick adobe walls of the Mission Solano chapel in Sonoma absorbed and muffled the restrained chatter of the excited guests as they flowed in to fill every dim corner of the old building. But when the ancient iron Mexican bell that hung out front began chiming, Santiago knew the time was near.

In the front of the narrow chapel, rows of pews were in place for the very closest members of the wedding party, Aunt Benecio seated one side of the aisle, Doña Valentina the other. The Russell men and their women, Francine and Antal and even Consuela, had found their places, Leo Carver being the only one who was conspicuously absent. Behind the old oak benches it was standing room only, and it appeared as if the whole town and more were crowded in to see Santiago Valaquez Mackinnon wed Josefa Martinez Stewart.

Among them were many who, like Santiago, paid homage to their shared Spanish heritage, clad in *gente de razón* thigh-hugging breeches that widened below the knees. Satin sashes in brilliant colors — red, black or, in Santiago's case, emerald green — looped waists thick and thin, to be glimpsed from under heavily embroidered and gold-braided jackets.

Santiago was pin-pricked by the jitters. Caleb would be entering through the oak-framed archway in the next few minutes, Josefa on his arm. In the absence of her father Fergus Stewart, who'd been dead nearly twenty years, her brother was doing the honors, giving the bride away.

He allowed himself a quick, private smile. The idea of anyone "giving the bride away" was so wide of the mark when applied to beautiful, strong-willed Josefa, a woman as likely to allow herself to be "given away" against her wishes as she was to drink cleaning fluid.

The bell's sonorous notes faded away. The excited cheers of children wafted into the dim interior, the sunlight filtering through the narrow iron-fretted windows along the side walls. A beam reflected on a silver plate balanced on the altar rail, where the two silver rings they would be exchanging in the next hour lay on white linen.

It was mid-June, the time early Americans called Full Strawberry Moon, when the first wild summer strawberries ripened, seen as a particularly auspicious for marriage.

This ceremony — the beginning of several days of partying — was open to anyone who wished to attend, and they'd come from far and wide to be there. Everyone sensed they were witnessing something historic: the mending of a family breach which had outlasted the lives of the principal players and deserved to be ended. All would relish the ensuing fiesta.

The chapel quieted and stilled, as if in response to a silent command, and the back of Santiago's neck prickled. He didn't need to swing around to know that Caleb and Josefa were poised in the entry. He heard the rustle of silk as the chapel's female audience swiveled, all eyes on the doorway to catch a first glimpse of the bride. He stared straight ahead, past Father Giovanni waiting in his richly braided priest's robes, fixing his eyes on the altar, on the sparkling light cast from the golden candlesticks, engraving this moment in his heart forever.

He could hear the soft footfalls as brother and sister advanced, and then Caleb was handing Josefa over, his face flushed with pride, and she was at his side, this woman he wanted to share the rest of his life with, looking even more glorious than he could ever have imagined.

Her eyes glowed with a joy she could not contain. Under the mist of white mantilla lace that tumbled from a high Spanish comb her face was radiant, a smile trembling on her finely curved lips. He clasped her hand and squeezed gently. "Mi amor," he whispered.

She carried a sweet-smelling bouquet of white Castilian roses, and the closeness of her, the waxy smoke of the altar candles, the cloud of incense that hung from the pre-service ministrations . . . For a few seconds the heaviness of the air threatened to overwhelm him.

The marriage preliminaries had been sparse and solemn. They'd both spent hours in the chapel at different times, praying about the responsibilities they were assuming to each other and their children. They were serious, committed, and prepared, he reminded himself, and he couldn't faint now.

Father Giovanni stepped forward with greetings, and the service was underway. Through the Bible readings, the responsorial Psalm, the alleluias and the Gospel, they moved with formal dignity to their vows, and it all flowed before him like an astounding dream.

They kneeled as an altar boy proffered Father Giovanni the silver plate that had caught Santiago's eye earlier, the plate carrying their two rings. The priest blessed them and slipped them onto their wedding fingers, then looped a scarf over their shoulders, joining them in a continuous circle, a second physical sign of their yoking together in matrimony.

With a loudly proclaimed "Dominus vobiscum" Father Giovanni, now smiling broadly, concluded the formalities. As if on cue, stringed instruments sounded the notes of a popular hymn, and an expectant wave of whispers and rustling swept through the watching crowd.

Santiago reverently peeled back the mist of lace and swept it back over Josefa's shoulders to reveal her lovely face. He gazed at her for a few seconds, brushed her forehead with his lips, and laced her arm into his for their first walk together, out into the sunshine, as man and wife.

Three hours later, after the throng had eaten a large meal and invited guests were finding any comfortable corner to take a siesta before the dancing commenced at sunset, a knot of well-wishers still lingered offering their salutations: "Saludos" and "Viva mil años." "Live a thousand years" and "God follow you."

They'd eaten stewed chicken, a beef hash mixed with scrambled eggs, onions, tomatoes well-seasoned with red chili peppers, beans with tortillas, salted pork and coriander frijoles, roast duck, sweet potatoes and lettuce salad. All washed down with Orleans vino del pais or juice, and sweets served with coffee. Now it was time to rest before the dancing.

Josefa looped her arm around Santiago's waist and felt a bolt of warmth shoot through her as he responded by drawing her closer to his side. She whispered in his ear, "It's time to go if I'm going to dance all night." The bride had to leave first, giving the guests permission to then also slip away.

"Mi querido." He pressed his lips to the side of her head. "You must be exhausted. You've been busy for days now, and you've ensured it's a wonderful success." He pressed his index finger to her lips. "You've made me the happiest man in the world."

She caught hold of his finger and kissed it. "It's hard to believe we've done it. Never in my wildest dreams . . ." Tears flooded her eyes, and she had to squeeze them shut to stop them overflowing. "Look at me. I don't know what you're doing to me. The happiest day of my life and I'm crying." She gave a self-conscious laugh. "It must be the baby."

He placed a gentle, protecting hand on her abdomen. "Blessed with a fruitful wife." He grinned. "How lucky can a man get?"

Josefa sank gratefully onto the soft bed in the quiet, shuttered room, already savoring the images from this day of all days. They'd been transported from the chapel to Francine and Antal's house in a garlanded bridal carreta drawn by two white oxen. Doña Valentina and Aunt Benecio and the rest of the family followed close behind in similar garlanded carts. Behind them rode relatives and friends on horseback, a noisy colorful cavalcade wending their way out of town to the Orleans Hills estate, a band of musicians accompanying the gay procession, singing their own ribald songs louder than they'd ever sung the hymns in church.

Horses impatient at the pace of the oxen pulling the carretas pawed the ground fretfully, raising dust clouds. Dashing caballeros caught up maidens to ride in front of them, the dun-colored habits and tiny-brimmed sugar-loaf hats of the equestriennes foils for the men's gay velvet suits. Metallic embroidery sparkled on their jackets; twisted silver shone from their sombreros.

And infused through it all, the smell of a hundred flowers, garlanded in the women's hair or pinned to their dresses, wilting in the sun, releasing their warm fragrance even as they faded.

The three-hour meal replete with toasts and compliments had pulsed with merriment, but now Josefa desperately needed to rest before the festivities resumed at dark, when the bride and groom were expected to dance until dawn.

"How could I have imagined, six months ago, that I would ever be this happy?" Josefa traced her finger down Santiago's firm tanned jaw. "When Rory died, I thought I would never be happy again."

Her heart still lurched in pain at his name, but it felt right somehow to speak it on this most wondrous of days.

Santiago took her hand and kissed her knuckles. "Ah, Rory. He'll always be with us." He stroked her head. "I hate it that he's not here to share this occasion with us. That I never got to know him as a brother while he was alive." He cupped her chin in his hand. "But for me to have the honor to have you as my wife . . . So much has happened in the six months since he died. And I suppose there's a very good chance we wouldn't be wed if he was still alive." He dipped his head, his expression momentarily bleak. "The thing I most want to make sure of now is that I care for his child as well as he would have."

Josefa rolled onto her back and adjusted the pillows behind her head. They'd retreated to the privacy of one of the Esterhazy's guest rooms for their siesta. After all the demands of the past few weeks, she cherished this rare time alone.

"Oh, Santiago, thanks to Aunt Benecio for being so wise about that. She really put me right there — although I know we nearly went off the rails over it."

She rolled to face him. The tenderness inside her threatened to spill over in tears again. She stared at him in a dazed delight. She was still finding it hard to believe she really had won this man as her lawful wedded husband.

"Strange, isn't it, how thanks to your own unhappy childhood, you've got such a good idea of what you don't want to repeat."

Santiago nuzzled the side of her face.

A laugh of wonder at her good fortune rippled up from deep inside. "And now, if I'm going to be dancing under that Full Strawberry Moon in a few hours, I really must sleep."

Tomorrow morning, after they had danced and entertained their guests all night, there would be the final seal on it all, the tossing of the cascarones, eggshells filled with silver and gold confetti or scented toilet water. Guests prepared ahead of time for this concluding storm of merriment, showering bride and groom — and one another — until everyone was spangled and drenched.

She gazed tenderly at the man lying next to her, already asleep, and imagined his handsome face, his long brown hair, messed and damp, the spangles on his fine cheekbones glistening. This man. Her husband.

THE END

Enjoy Hope Redeemed? Get Of Gold & Blood Boxed Set, Books #1-3

If you've enjoyed Hope Redeemed why not jump into the Of Gold & Blood book bundle – Books 1 – 3 in the series, 1000+ pages of heart-wrenching romance and pulse-pounding suspense! In California's Gilded Age, all that glitters can be love... or murder.

California, 1868. The three Russell brothers have been separated by time and tragedy. When they reunite in a proverbial promised land, they must heal the past and build a future for themselves and the strong women who hold their hearts. But the rough pioneer frontier breeds more danger than delight...

The Russell clan continues to find themselves at the center of mysterious deaths and murderous adversaries. Unwilling to let corruption ruin their dreams of a prosperous future, can they solve these deadly crimes before they're fitted for their own pine boxes?

The *Of Gold & Blood* bundle features the first three books in this historical mystery series. If you like enduring romance, captivating characters, and edge-of-your-seat suspense, then you'll love Jenny Wheeler's compelling page-turners.

Enjoy this book? You Can Make a Difference

Reviews are the most powerful tools in my kit when it comes to getting my books noticed. Much as I'd love it, I don't have the budget of a big publisher to buy bill board ads and other national advertising. But I have the promise of something more powerful – something publishers envy. And that's a committed and loyal bunch of readers. Honest reviews of my books help them gain the attention of others who might appreciate them too.

Post Your Reviews Here:
For Amazon: https://geni.us/elG8
For Goodreads: https://bit.ly/2WCTVg1

ACKNOWLEDGMENTS

Once again, I wish to voice by warmest thanks to the staff at Birkenhead Library, my local library, where I always find ready support and great service.

I am indebted to the New Zealand Library Interloan facility for arranging access to reference titles not generally available, and to the services of C.J. Simmons, Interloan & Information Supply Librarian. In particular I owe a huge "Thank You" to Professor Ann Twinam, Professor of History, Walter Prescott Webb Chair in History, University of Texas at Austin and author of *Public Lives, Private Secrets: Gender, Honor, Sexuality, and Illegitimacy in Colonial Spanish America*.

'Public Lives, Private Secrets' outlined in detail the complicated practices governing colonial Spain's treatment of children born either out of wedlock or in other unconventional circumstances. Not only was it invaluable as I worked on my character Santiago's story, but Professor Twinam generously replied to my emails seeking clarification on some issues. Of course, if I have interpreted her material incorrectly I apologize in advance and accept full responsibility, but I am very grateful for her personal assistance.

Two other delightful books sourced through the same facility gave me first person accounts of courtship and marriage in early California. They were *A Scotch Paisano in Old Los Angeles, Hugo Reid's Life in California, 1832 – 52 Derived from his correspondence,* by Susanna Bryant Dakin, and *The Lives of William Hartnell,* by the same author.

I am once again indebted to the great team of people who have helped me publish this Book #6 in the Of Gold & Blood series. They include copy editor Stephen Stratford, proof editor Nikki Crutchley, and the faithful readers who assisted with reading early editions and giving feedback and reviews.

ABOUT THE AUTHOR

Jenny Wheeler is the author of the Of Gold & Blood Old California mystery series:

Poisoned Legacy #1.
Brother Betrayed #2.
Double Jeopardy #3.
Tangled Destiny (Christmas novella and Prequel.) #4
Unbridled Vengeance #5
Hope Redeemed, A Spanish Novella, #6
Boxed Set/Book Bundle Of Gold & Blood, Books 1 – 3.

Jenny's online home is at jennywheeler.biz or email
Jenny@jennywheeler.biz
You can connect with Jenny on:
Facebook: @JennyWheeler.Biz
Twitter: @Jenny_Biz
Instagram: @jennysbingereading
Pinterest www.pinterest.nz/jennywheelbooks/
Goodreads: goodreads.com/author/show/11371547.Jenny_Wheeler
Bookbub: www.bookbub.com/profile/jenny-wheeler